BE MINE THIS CHRISTMAS NIGHT

STAR LIGHT ~ STAR BRIGHT SERIES BOOK ONE

L. A. SARTOR

Star Light, Star bright,
The first star I see tonight,
I wish I may, I wish I might,
Have the wish I wish tonight.

~ anonymous

This story begged to be written because Christmas has always held a special place in my heart.

For my brother, Jim, because I remember all those wonderful Christmas mornings we shared. I love you.

And always for my husband, Gary, who makes it all possible. I will always love you.

1

———

GLANCING AT THE CROWD BUNDLED UP AGAINST THE NEAR zero-degree December evening as they gathered in the street, on the sidewalk, the neighbor's yards—wherever there was room—Annabelle Hamilton grinned. She loved the anticipation building toward the moment the thousands of lights adorning her home would be turned on.

Showtime.

With her hand on the switch, she scanned the crowd one more time and caught sight of a small, solitary figure standing outside the house of her new next-door neighbor.

She knew two young boys lived there, so perhaps he was one the kids. But why was the house dark when she was sure everyone was home and it was far too early for the boys to be in bed? And why didn't he just come over, instead of hiding in the shadows?

"Annie? Everyone is waiting."

The nudge on her shoulder from one of the twin

brothers who helped her hang the thousands of lights pulled her attention back to the big moment.

"Sorry. See that kid over there?" Annie pointed, but the child had left.

Shaking away her puzzlement, she held her breath and flipped the electrical switch.

The ooohs and ahhhs reflected her own thrill at seeing the brilliant magic of light sparkling everywhere. Especially the huge stars that arrived special delivery a few hours ago. The twins had worked feverishly to get them hung, and the stars were spectacular, glimmering high in the tall linden, looking as if they'd just fallen from the sky to hover in her tree.

The applause started and swelled, and someone in the crowd began singing the Christmas carol "Joy to the World." Annie joined in, belting it out for all she was worth.

Her daddy established this tradition of decorating with lights on one particularly rough Christmas as a way to cheer her up, and it worked. Every Christmas since that long-ago year, hope symbolized by light had been a part of her celebration. Even when she lived in the old homestead in the backwoods of Maine and she was the only person around to enjoy her effort. Just her and the critters.

She turned back to look at her home of the last four years, nestled close to Chautauqua Park in Boulder, Colorado. The tingle of pride, followed by the warm contentment she always felt when pulling into the driveway, was magnified tonight.

The steep eaves were defined by miniature white

lights, while the bushes and trees out front and in her backyard were strung with hundreds more of the little bulbs.

Just before she ducked under the peaked roof of her carport to begin ladling the hot cider bubbling in the crock pot, Annie glanced once more at the dark house next door.

Her neighbor had moved in more than a month ago, and by the buff look of him, she figured he was some sort of pro athlete or maybe a sports manager.

From her second-floor bedroom window, she'd unabashedly watched him flex and lift as the pile of boxes from the U-Haul dwindled. Sweat glistened on his forehead even in the winter chill. The next time he came out of the house, a sweat band held back his ebony hair, and he'd pulled off his sweatshirt, revealing a gray T-shirt with cutoff sleeves, the front emblazoned with a faded "Black's Gym, Chantilly, Virginia" emblem.

Another man was traipsing in and out of the house, spending most of his time helping the kids with their smaller boxes or keeping them out of the way of the hunk. Annie wondered who the second man was.

And the boys, they were adorable. She'd guess they were around seven and nine, and she couldn't wait to meet them properly.

Probably not tonight, she regretted, glancing again at the dark windows. Maybe they'd gone to bed early to avoid the chaos. But chaos was part of the lighting celebration, and she'd made a point of putting a flier in her new neighbor's mailbox announcing her "Annual Christmas Lighting" dates and the warning that the lights were on from dusk to dawn.

So maybe he hated Christmas lights, but Annie would bet her bottom dollar those boys would have been as entranced by the lights as she'd been when she was a wee girl and her daddy turned them on each season.

A collective cheer went up from the crowd as the surly gray clouds that had been gathering and building all day finally let loose their treasure of white fluffy flakes.

She moved from underneath the shelter of the carport and looked upward, letting the cold flakes land on her face. "Thanks, Daddy," she whispered.

"Who are you talking to?"

Annie glanced down to see which of the many neighborhood kids was addressing her, surprised to find it was the younger of the two boys from next door.

She looked at the house, the lights still dark. Maybe he'd been the one standing alone in the shadows. Which meant his father most likely didn't know he was outside in the frigid cold.

Guiding him under the carport to the cider table and a bit of warmth, Annie chose her answer carefully. "I was just saying thanks to my daddy for sending the snow."

"Is he in heaven?"

"I like to think of him sitting on a star high in the sky, so yes, if that's heaven, that's where he is."

"My mommy's in heaven too, but I don't think she's on a star. I don't know where she is."

Annie hadn't realized the man next door was a widower. "Has your mommy been gone long?"

"Forever."

"Two years, Josh. Don't exaggerate."

Annie spun to her left to see her new neighbor in his buttoned-up black wool overcoat, complete with a dark gray muffler wrapped around his neck, looming over the table, irritation written all over his face.

"Excuse me, but would you mind moving a bit farther to your left?" she asked.

He looked baffled at her request, and she didn't care that she was less than polite—his brusque answer to his son instantly raised her hackles.

COLE EVANS TOOK IN THE MIGHTY MOUSE IN FRONT OF HIM, his son's crestfallen face, the line forming behind him and stepped left.

"Thank you," mighty mouse said, not bothering to look at him.

His petite neighbor handed a steaming cup of cider to an elderly woman he'd seen around the neighborhood once or twice since moving in. Then a couple of kids got cups carefully filled only halfway so that the hot liquid wouldn't spill and burn them if they jiggled the cup.

Something he'd never have thought about, and Lauren would have. His brother-in-law, Mitch, was right—Cole did need him to help while he learned how to be a solo parent.

"Would you like some?"

His neighbor was offering Josh cider, but not him. Cole

grinned, he couldn't help it. Somehow, he'd made her mad, and they'd not even formally met. Yet.

Josh looked at him for permission to accept the cider, and he nodded.

After his son finished drinking from his carefully cradled cup, Cole figured it was time to introduce himself and make a graceful exit out of the crush of people gawking at the light display. It reminded him of a play opening on Broadway. Not at all what he'd expected when he learned an author lived next door.

He thought of authors as solitary people, living in their own world, creating characters, playing with their lives, and maybe giving them a happy ending.

He extended his hand. "I'm Dr. Cole Evans and this is my younger son, Josh."

The petite woman in front of him stared like he'd grown two heads. What had he said?

"Author Annabelle Hamilton."

Ah, the whole formal name thing, complete with his PhD. He had to remember where he was living now, the part of the country where that kind of formality was reserved for colleagues, and usually only for the first introduction.

He lowered his hand. "Oh, sorry, it's an East Coast thing."

"Chantilly, Virginia?"

"How did you know that?"

"Your gym T-shirt."

As soon as the words left her lips, her eyes widened and her gaze flew to his.

Why? When had he last worn his gym shirt outside? Moving in.

His smile broadened. She immediately looked away him, obviously embarrassed by her revelation. Cole followed her gaze to see Josh staring at her, bug-eyed.

"Are you the star books lady?"

No, please no. Cole closed his eyes. A hard lump tightened his throat at his son's wistful question.

Josh adored those books. Lauren had read one or another of the dozens of short books to him every night. For a while after Lauren died, Cole tried to keep up the ritual, but work kept him coming home later and later, and often Josh was asleep.

His son wouldn't let their housekeeper read to him, and Mitch didn't pick up the practice. Every once in a while, Cole would find a book tucked in the sheets when he woke his son. A reminder of how much they'd all lost when Lauren died.

Cole refocused on the present.

Annabelle bent so she could be face to face with his son. "Yes, I'm the star books lady. Do you read my books?"

"Some of them. Some are too hard."

"Well, I can help you with the words, so come on over any time."

"Really?"

"Yup. And, Josh, call me Annie, okay? Although I'm thinking being called 'star books lady' is pretty darn cool."

The woman hadn't bothered to glance Cole's way again after she'd inadvertently revealed her peeping. And now she was issuing invitations to his son without his consent? *And when did that start to be an issue with you?*

Just now.

Damn.

The mighty mouse standing in from of him was no doubt a very pretty lady, especially with a thousand twinkling lights highlighting those reddish tints in her short dark hair. The bulky parka did nothing to diminish her petite figure, and her eyes reminded him of the rich whiskey he and Mitch often drank once the boys were asleep.

Stop cataloging her features. You're not going there, remember?

But he didn't want her to start being buddies with his son.

Why?

Because she's a woman.

Well, that's just stupid.

Cole turned to his son, using him as an excuse to get the heck away. "Time to go."

"Aw, Dad, just a little bit longer," Josh pleaded.

"Son, you left the house without permission, so no. And according to the flier Ms. Hamilton left us, you'll be able to see the lights until New Year's," he said, knowing his tone was a bit too sharp and his son would cajole him daily about seeing either Annie or the lights.

Damn.

"Do you have a problem with that?" Annabelle asked.

Cole raised a brow at the challenge in her voice.

"No, I'm a believer in blackout curtains."

ANNIE'S JAW DROPPED, AND IT WAS ONLY AFTER DR. COLE Evans and Josh had reached the end of her driveway that she thought of a good comeback. "I've heard vampires sleep like that," she muttered.

The arrogance of the man.

Just then Jenny Malone, her best friend and the reason she moved to Boulder, burst onto the scene.

"Who's a vampire? I'm sorry I'm late—the traffic backed up on 36 the minute the flakes began falling. Who was the good-looking man that just stormed out of here?"

Annie smiled at Jen's non-stop run of words. Irrepressible and a brilliant digital forensic expert, Jen was constantly on the go, and unless it was business, she was always ten to fifteen minutes late.

"The vampire."

At Jenny's quizzical look, Annie told the truth. "That was my new neighbor."

"Seriously? Wow. What did you do to put a scowl on that gorgeous face?"

"Why would you think I'd done something?"

Annie grinned at her friend's raised brow. "Celebrate the season with lights? Be an author his son loves? Be a woman? I have no idea."

Jenny pursed her lips and started ladling out the cider, taking the job from Annie.

As Annie left the cover of the carport to mingle and enjoy the lights, she called back, "And he's a widower," smiling wider when Jen's eyes grew large and her friend waggled her brows.

Despite Jenny's obvious insinuation that her neighbor was yummy and maybe available, Annie had no intention of finding out. Josh was adorable, and she'd love having him visit, but Cole? Not so much.

Anyway, it was obvious that *Dr. Cole Evans* was enamored of his medical degree and its status. She wasn't. Her daddy had always been known as Doc Hamilton and was introduced that way by people who knew him, but she'd never heard him introduce himself any other way than Adam Hamilton.

Annie stopped thinking about her neighbor and recaptured the feeling of wonder as she walked among the crowds, admiring her celebration of the season.

Finally the cars blocking the street began to thin, and Jenny joined her as she walked across the road to enjoy her lights from a distance. The stark difference between her lighted wonderland and Cole Evans's house was unsettling.

Maybe they didn't celebrate Christmas, but then, her lights weren't strictly about Christmas—more about the peace and hope of the holiday.

The snow fell harder, and Annie let it lay on her jacket and hair where it landed, relishing the essence of winter. She'd spent a year in Florida and missed Colorado's diverse changing of the seasons.

She swiftly considered the merits of each season. After it snowed, winter's short days were often sun-kissed because of Boulder's high altitude.

Spring and its indecision of whether it was winter or summer as the crocus emerged—the first harbingers of the new season—only to have snow blanketing them the next day.

Summer with temps high enough for tubing in Boulder Creek, intensely blue skies, shorts, riding a bike and homemade lime popsicles.

And with fall came the expectancy of the winter, yet the remnants of summer still lifted the temperatures so the days often made wearing shorts still in order.

Yes, she loved all the seasons, but as she admired her lights, Annie admitted winter and Christmas had the edge.

A light flickered on in a room at the Evans' household, drawing her attention. A small figure stood at the window, blackout curtains pulled aside, looking toward her house.

Josh probably couldn't see her standing across the street, but she saw him for a second as the lights of her house played on his face, and the yearning written there tore at her heart.

The lights went off, and the curtain dropped as Josh abruptly turned around, apparently caught in the act.

"Too bad," she murmured.

"What?" Jenny asked.

"Josh, the vampire's youngest son. He seems to really want to—" Annie stamped her cold feet, now getting numb as she searched to find the right words.

"He wants to be a part of this, of Christmas, and his father seems to be trying to make sure he doesn't."

She braved Jenny's stare, then turned to match it. "To quote you, 'What?'"

"Don't start with them. If the father is a widower, and the boy—or at least the little one—misses the mother horribly, then getting involved with the son will only bring you heartache. Face it, kiddo, you're not their mother. And it won't bring the father to your side either."

"I don't want the father, but I do want Josh to enjoy the season."

"I'm warning you, it's trouble."

Annie slipped her hand through her friend's arm and headed back to her house. "Time for a glass of wine. I want to show you my new story."

"You're changing the subject, but I'm up for wine. Just remember, you're going to make trouble if you get involved."

_____

COLE SAT AT HIS BREAKFAST TABLE, NURSING HIS SECOND mug of coffee. Weekends, when Lauren always made sure there was a fancy hot breakfast, were the worst. It had been their family time. From reading the paper in bed as the boys played with their iPads to afternoons spent walking one of the trails in the vast Ellanor Lawrence Park and finishing with homemade pizza or pasta for dinner.

Today, unless Mitch arrived soon, there would be cold cereal and maybe video games for the boys, more coffee and his home office for him.

And if Mitch did arrive, Cole thought he'd brave the snow and head to his lab up on the mesa above Boulder.

Funny, last night while talking to Annabelle, he'd had the oddest sense that she thought he was a medical doctor when he introduced himself as Dr. Cole Evans. And at the time he hadn't corrected her.

He studied the clouds, the atmosphere, not people and illness.

"Second cup already? How long have you been up?"

Cole hadn't heard his brother-in-law enter the room. He looked up, giving him a bleary grin. Mitchell Thomas grinned back, looking most like Lauren when he did that.

His blue eyes lit up as hers had. Their wide-open smiles were nearly identical, and while Mitch's sandy brown hair was showing premature gray at the temples, Lauren had made sure no gray ever showed on her head. Mitch was taller than his five-foot-eight sister by four inches.

Cole braced for the emptiness to bite him, and when it did, it bit a little less deep this morning. Nothing had changed except that he'd met his neighbor last night.

"I've been up most the night, had an interesting confrontation with the neighbor next door."

"You don't confront."

The subtext wasn't lost on Cole, and while he ignored the comment, he knew Mitch was right. Cole hadn't insisted that Lauren needed to see the doctor until she was too sick not to go.

And by then, learning she'd have to wait two to five years for a matching cadaver donor was no longer an option.

Both he and Mitch had offered themselves as live donors, and Lauren had at first refused, then reluctantly accepted Mitch's offer, telling Cole through tears and fear for her children that he might need to save his kidney for one of the boys, if the cancer was genetic in nature.

Mitch had positive cross-matched for the donation, which at first sounded great, but turned out the exact opposite. It was Lauren's choice to undergo the lengthy process of plasmapheresis to remove the antibodies in her blood that would have caused immediate rejection of Mitch's kidney.

Nobody anticipated the cascading failure of her organs.

Cole's thoughts took him back farther. It had been Mitch and Lauren together fighting the system and the social workers for as long as Cole could remember. His parents had taken the pair of them in until they were old enough and beyond the system's reach.

Mitch headed off to a full scholarship at Radford U while he and Lauren went to George Mason. And during those years, he and Lauren became a couple.

Cole's worry over Mitch's objecting to their new relationship was unfounded. After Cole was accepted to MIT for his PhD, he and Lauren were married, with Mitch as their best man.

Lauren soon became pregnant with Peter. Still Cole never thought of himself, Lauren and Mitch as anything other than a trio—maybe not the same as when they were all in high school, but a trio nonetheless, until Lauren's illness.

Everything changed then.

Cole blinked back the wetness in his eyes, coming back to the moment. He knew Mitch was still taunting him two years later because his brother-in-law hadn't healed from the pain of losing his sister. It was as raw as the day she died.

Yet only today had Cole felt his own slight lessening.

Why? Because he was having to confront Lauren's death on a different level? Did Josh's admiration of the "star books lady" have anything to do with this?

Cole loosened his grip on the coffee mug's handle and focused on Mitch and his zinger about confrontation.

"Oddly, last night I did just that. Confront," Cole said.

Peter bounded into the kitchen, iPad in hand. "Dad, I just found a patch of eight diamonds today on Minecraft. Hi, Uncle Mitch, what's for breakfast today? And after, can we go out and try those snowshoes? I think over a foot fell last night."

"Uncle Mitch, guess who we met last night?" Josh came into the kitchen, carrying a load of books.

Oh no.

At Mitch's glance, Cole shrugged, worried that he'd spoken the words aloud.

"Who?"

Josh turned the book over and pointed at a picture of Annabelle Hamilton. "Her. She lives right next door."

Cole met Mitch's gaze, and they shared the silent groan.

The intrusive noise of a machine drew Cole to the window.

Speak of the devil. Annie was pushing a snowblower the size of a small car up the sidewalk.

Mitch joined him at the window. "Who is that?"

"Annabelle Hamilton."

Josh hurried over, and Cole rolled his eyes. "*I* was going to scrape the sidewalk when I cleaned off the car to head to the lab today."

"You're going to work? We were going to get the Christmas tree today." Josh's voice was wounded.

"We can get the tree and try out those snowshoes, then your dad can help us decorate tonight," Mitch said.

Cole pulled on a heavy sweatshirt and put on his boots.

"Hey, we haven't had breakfast yet. Where are you going?" Peter asked, looking up from his iPad.

"I'm going to tell Ms. Hamilton she doesn't need to clear our sidewalk."

"Can I come talk to her too, Dad?" Josh asked.

"Later, son. I need to have a private talk with her."

MANNHEIM STEAMROLLER PLAYED THROUGH ANNIE'S earbuds from the MP3 player tucked into her parka pocket. What a glorious morning. The storm had moved on, the sky was brilliantly blue, and the sun sparkled off the pristine white blanket that covered everything.

Three weeks before Christmas and the snow was a foot deep. The forecasters predicted more this week, so Annie decided it was a sign they'd have a white Christmas. Not rational as that date was too many days away to forecast the weather, but she didn't care. Sometimes you just had to believe.

She stopped pushing the snowblower for a moment, catching her breath, leaning against the heavy machine. The weight of the snow-spewing monster on top of no sleep last night took its toll far sooner than normal.

She'd bought the biggest snowblower she could

handle, not only because of her wide driveway, but also, once she got going, the whole sidewalk on her side of the street got the Annie treatment.

And it was good exercise, especially when she knew she was going to make her favorite coffee as a treat afterward.

Taking a deep, frosty breath, Annie turned back to resume her task and jumped a foot when *Doctor* Cole Evans stood right in front of her machine, lips moving.

A chuckle bubbled up and despite her best intention, laughter escaped just as she pulled the earbuds from beneath her cap.

The furrow between his dark brows grew deeper. Annie grasped the handles of the snowblower tighter, fighting the urge to push him into the snow. He needed to lighten up.

"Jeeze, scare me to death. I'm sorry I didn't see you come up, but I was listening to music." She held one earbud closer to his ears so he could hear the Christmas music. If he didn't believe in Christmas, then she was taunting him, and somehow that didn't bother her a bit. Not her normal behavior, but the guy just seemed to push her ornery buttons.

"You don't have to clear our walk. I was going to do it when I came out to clean off the Pilot before I headed for the lab."

"I don't mind—it's good exercise so I can make myself a mocha peppermint coffee topped with whipped cream afterward. What kind of doctor are you that you have a lab?"

"An atmospheric physicist."

Annie's jaw dropped, then she laughed to cover her own astonishment as well as her embarrassment. "Not an MD, then. My mistake."

"Not in a million years. I faint at the sight of blood and anyone will tell you I've got no bedside manner."

"You got that right," she murmured under her breath.

"I'm sorry, what was that?"

"Nothing. Really, I plow the neighbor's walks all the time and it's fun, honest," she said, seeing his skeptical gaze. "You have snow in Virginia, don't you?"

"Of course. The wet slushy kind."

"So you had to remove that, right?"

"Right."

"No different."

"Except you're doing my sidewalk."

"I'm a simple author who does sidewalks on the side, okay?"

He snorted and she loved that he would do so. It was such a plebeian thing to do. Not at all "East Coast."

"Not a simple author. As you may have guessed, Josh loves your books. And having you live next door may be a curse to you."

"Never. I love kids."

"It's evident in your writing."

Not quite believing her ears, she stared at the man standing in front of her. "Why I do believe that's a compliment, which, before you can retract, I'll take," she added swiftly, seeing his mouth open, then shut.

"What are Josh and his brother doing this afternoon?

I've got a new character to illustrate and I'd love their input."

"Mitch is taking them Christmas tree shopping, then onto snow shoeing lessons this afternoon."

"Oh. Well that sounds like fun. Who is—"

Annie glanced up as Cole's front door opened. *And when did you start thinking of him as Cole instead of Doctor Cole Evans?*

The man Annie had seen helping Cole move in stood in the doorway, zipped his parka, and turned back in apparent surprise as Josh pushed past him.

"Annie, we're going Christmas tree shopping. Want to come?"

Cole froze as did the man at the door.

"Hey, Josh."

Without stopping to think, Annie hugged the boy after he ran right up to her.

"Want to introduce me to your brother and friend?" Annie nodded to the man and boy who now stood next to Cole.

"Oh. That's Uncle Mitch. And that," he said, pointing to the youngest in the trio of males standing together, "is my brother, Peter."

Peter stood unmoving and unsmiling until "Uncle Mitch" nudged him. Not Cole, Annie realized, but Mitch. Curious.

Peter looked at Mitch, then at her. "Ah, nice to meet you."

Annie smiled at Peter and held out her hand to Mitch.

"And nice to meet you both as well. It's great Cole has a brother nearby."

"I'm Lauren's brother."

Ah. More curious. "My mistake." It was evident by Mitch's clipped tones he didn't like her. He didn't know her at all, but he sure didn't like her already. And that she wasn't invited to their outing was also pretty darn clear.

She turned to Josh. "I'm sorry I can't come with you. It sounds like fun, but I'm working on illustrating a new character today and my deadline is getting much too close. I can't believe I agreed to a January fifth date. Must have been crazy. Anyway, have fun—it's a great day to be outside."

She saw Josh's pout. At least she'd made one friend next door. Cole had actually bent a little today, Peter was polite when prodded, and Mitch's subtext was clear as a bell.

Three out of four males were going to be cool or frigid toward her.

Not understanding why that would be the case, and upset that she cared one iota, she started up the machine, struggled to turn it around, waving away Cole's offer of assistance, and headed down the block, away from them.

As she plowed the sidewalk down the steep hill, she gnawed her bottom lip, wondering why she was fretting about those men.

Slipping on a patch of snow-covered ice, Annie went down hard, the snowblower still running, showering her with snow.

Tired of staring at the blank computer monitor sitting on his basic government-issue desk, Cole pushed his chair away from the screen that had remained stubbornly empty of new equations since he'd reached his office at NCAR.

Moving outside onto the small balcony jutting from one of the many tall columns of labs and offices, Cole again admired the scientific complex built on Table Mesa. The sandstone-textured concrete buildings of the iconic National Center for Atmospheric Research were an I. M. Pei design, inspired by the geometric forms of Anasazi cliff dwellings. The structures blended in well with the massive sandstone Flatirons that were so emblematic of Boulder.

Cole had visited NCAR several times for meetings and envied the energy he'd felt permeating the air, so when the director had asked him to move his research and team to Boulder, he jumped at the chance.

Additionally, Mitch lived here.

His brother-in-law had offered many times to move to Virginia and help with the boys, stressing that his web design business was completely portable, but his offer was too much for Cole to accept.

Now, after moving here, he admitted that Mitch *was* the perfect solution to helping with the boys.

As Cole stared at the city below him, his thoughts shifted to the real reason he couldn't concentrate today. Instead of the new severe-weather tracking and prediction models he should be working on, he was focused on one house, one woman.

He replayed the scene from this morning as he watched in horror when Annie slipped and fell, Josh's scream a ghastly punctuation mark. His son reached her first. Cole got there a split second later and turned off the snowblower, relieved as Annie tried to sit up.

Thank goodness she had on a thick woolen cap—she'd hit the pavement pretty hard.

Refusing any help other than getting her snowblower back to the carport, Annie entered her house and firmly shut the door behind her.

Cole couldn't banish the guilt swirling through him. Annie had been nothing but kind and generous, at least to Josh. But Cole was man enough to admit he hadn't been particularly friendly when her attention briefly focused on him.

Suddenly knowing what he wanted to do, he left the small balcony and returned to the warmth of his office. He quickly shut down the computer and locked the door behind him. Soon he was heading home with one stop to make first.

And less than forty-five minutes later, balancing the cardboard tray with its two Starbucks paper cups in one hand, Cole pressed the doorbell on Annie's home.

No answer. He pressed it again, suddenly worried that her fall was worse than she let on and she'd gone to urgent care or worse, the hospital.

Just as Cole was about to set the tray of coffees down and make a call to Boulder Community Hospital to check, the door swung open. Annie stood there, giving a good impression of a sleep-tousled nymph.

Her short dark hair stood at all angles. She wore navy leggings, a green, baggy long-sleeved T-shirt, and thick white woolen socks. Framed in the large doorway, she looked vulnerable, and the urge to enfold her in a hug surprised him.

"Dr. Evans, what brings you here?"

No doubt about it, Cole deserved the chill in her voice. He thrust the tray toward her. "Peace offering, but it seems I've woken you."

"I was napping, but it's time to get up. Sometimes I work until the wee hours of the morning, and last night was one of them. When we met this morning, I hadn't yet been to bed." She bent closer to the tray and sniffed. "Are those mocha peppermint lattes?"

"Didn't you say those were your favorite?"

"I did, and you have two. Would you like to come in and drink yours?"

Why hadn't he noticed her smile before? It lit her face, triggering a grin from him, if for no other reason than because when her smile reached her eyes, it was contagious. *Damn.*

"Thank you," he said. "I would. I need to talk to you."

Her smile faded. "Is this a bribe?" She wiggled her cup at him.

"No, as I said, a simple peace offering."

Dusk was falling fast, and suddenly the lights blazed on in her front yard, startling Cole.

Annie smiled wider this time. "Oh-oh, the lights. Are you going to run away again?"

"Is that what you think I was doing?"

"I don't know. I got the distinct impression you didn't approve of the display, or maybe shied away from light in general."

Her eyes twinkled with mischief, and he felt he was missing the joke. "No, it wasn't that at all."

Finally, Annie moved back, allowing him entrance to her home.

He stepped into her foyer. The high-pitched fir ceiling echoed the outline of the steep eaves out front. The pecan tone of the wood and the brick-laid entry gave off an immediate essence of warmth and comfort.

Following Annie into the great room was a feast for the eyes. From this angle she looked way too curvy and tantalizing as her trim legs disappeared into the over-sized shirt, giving his libido an uneasy jolt.

And when he could pull his gaze from Annie's backside, the house itself drew him. Craftsman-style furniture grouped in several seating arrangements gave a sense of intimacy for conversation yet still felt like being part of the entire crowd the large room could easily handle.

The plastered walls painted in a soft vanilla created a wonderful canvas for the many dark-framed oil paintings that graced the walls.

"Who is Adam Hamilton?" he asked, reading the bold slash signing the pieces.

"My father. He was a great painter and a gifted physician."

"I agree. These look like Maine the way I remember it, both the seascapes and the winter scenes."

That earned him a smile from her. All of what he said was true. The paintings were superb.

Cole turned to the lit fireplace, immediately mesmerized by the tiny fingers of flames shooting through a sea of crushed glass.

Annie chose a chair sitting diagonally to the fire, facing what must be a fifteen-foot Christmas tree, decorated in a charming mishmash of style and ornaments.

Somehow he'd expected an overwhelming display of Santas and angels and other obvious Christmas themes, but she only had the tree.

And it worked. It wasn't glitzy or designer driven, it felt like Annie. *And just what do you know about Annie? Nothing.*

Not totally true.

"What did you want to talk to me about?"

He locked gazes with her. Annie's eyes held that hint of mischief, a bit of curiosity, and a lot of wary.

3

"IT'S ABOUT JOSH."

Annie blinked. Cole made those three words sound so dramatic. What on earth could be wrong with Josh? If he were sick, this wouldn't be a social call.

"He's already really taken with you because of the books—"

"And that's a problem because?" She was deeply disappointed that he thought he needed to warn her about his still-grieving son.

Cole looked a bit uncomfortable, and she decided to quit baiting the poor man. Obviously he really wasn't good at these one-on-one interactions.

"It's not a problem, yet. Lauren, my wife, used to read him one or another every night and since she's been gone... I just thought you should know he's really keen on spending time here, and if he becomes a nuisance, then you have to let me or Mitch know."

"Nuisance?" Annie set down her cup, leaning forward

on her elbows and forgetting her pledge to give the man in front of her a break. "Cole, first off, Josh could never be a nuisance. I adore kids and your son is no exception. And I know after Christmas holidays are over, he'll be too busy when he goes back to school to have free time to spend over here, so I meant it when I said he could come over."

Cole leaned back as if trying to escape her words. She leaned forward even more. "And what is this with Mitch?"

"What do you mean, 'with Mitch'?"

The immediate temperature drop in the room had nothing to do with the weather. Well, too bad, he came to her to talk. They were on her turf, and she could talk about whatever she wanted to. "I noticed this morning that it was Mitch who touched Peter on the back as a politeness reminder, not you. And now you tell me to talk to Mitch about your son. If," she stressed the word, "I need to talk to anyone about Josh, it will only be to you."

Braving Cole's assessing gaze, she picked up her latte and took another sip, nodding with appreciation as the mocha and mint slid over her tongue.

Instead of addressing the point she'd just made, Cole rose and moved to study the Christmas tree. Annie watched over the rim of her cup as he touched one, then another of the ornaments. A gentle touch, with his long, lean fingers just skimming over the miniature wooden sled or a dough-wreath bedecked with glitter. Then he found her first star.

The first character of her *Star Light, Star Bright* books. Her father, as ill as he'd been, had carved it from wood and taken it to Bangor to have the small star gilded. "That's Alpha."

He turned, surprising her with a smile when she expected a frown after her fervent declaration about Josh. "I guessed that, from *Big Star, Little Boy*. And this one must be Suri?"

"Right. Odd."

"What?" he asked.

"I didn't think you'd know the book's characters."

"I don't know much, that was Lauren's department, but when a new book of yours came out, Josh would ask to have it read every night. Then he'd recite parts of it later."

Annie studied Cole as he walked around the tree, leaning in to get a closer look when an ornament caught his attention. She imagined him studying his instruments with the same precision.

"How long does it take you to decorate this?"

"Not long. I have a decorating party, Jenny comes with her boyfriend du jour, and I invite a few other people. Between the wine, food, joking and fifteen or so bodies, it takes one evening. Now, taking it down takes a couple of days."

"I can imagine." For the second time, his smile reached his blue eyes, the skin crinkling at the corners in a delightfully appealing way. A real smile, not simply a polite one.

The room temperature swung suddenly to the hot side, the climb entirely due to the man standing at the tree. Something she hadn't expected or, frankly, wanted.

Liar. You've been thinking of embracing that concept of friends-with-benefits, so why not with Cole?

Annie drank deeply from her cup, trying to get that thought and all it entailed out of her head, and swallowed too quickly.

Choking on the hot liquid, she felt a hand thumping her back. Waving Cole away, she fought the spasm and finally it disappeared.

"Thanks. Anyway, back to Josh, I don't think it's going to be a problem," she said.

"I hope you're right. He could be looking for a mother figure."

"Again, no problem there—motherhood isn't in my forecast."

Cole looked at her oddly, which was okay. She wasn't going into deep revelations with the man, now or later, especially if she got into a strictly physical relationship with him.

"Peculiar thing to say from someone who obviously gets along with and understands children as much as you."

"Again a compliment. Thank you," Annie said, ignoring the first part of the sentence and hoping he'd get the hint that the subject wasn't open for discussion.

The doorbell chimed.

Annie jumped up to open it, and Mitch stood there with a scowl on his face.

Wonderful.

"Is Cole here?"

"Mitch, nice to see you. Welcome to my home. Come in —we're having the lattes Cole brought. Wasn't that nice of him? He was checking up on me. So neighborly of him." The imp in her wanted him to know that at least she and Cole were on speaking terms, *and* that they were on her turf.

He stepped through the door but didn't follow her past the foyer. "Cole, pizzas are on their way. I thought you'd want to know."

Cole placed his cup on the coffee table and stood, yet made no move toward the door.

Neither man asked her to join them for dinner, and an uncomfortable silence filled the air. Annie waited another minute just to see what would happen, even though the hostess in her knew she should step in and fill the breach.

She wasn't expecting to be asked, but it was evident Mitch had taken a dislike to her and she wasn't about to let that come between her and Josh, or even Peter if she could help it.

Seconds passed and now the silence was getting silly. "Cole, thanks for the latte. It was nice of you to check up on me. Enjoy the pizza and tell the boys hi from me."

Cole followed only when she led the way to the door. "Oh, and there should be another crowd tonight for the lights. I'll have cider again in about an hour if the boys want to come over."

"Would you like to join us for dinner?" Cole asked. "I make a mean cheater salad."

"Cheater salad?"

"From a bag. But I do make the dressing from scratch."

"Someday I'll have to try it, but tonight, I'm on cider

duty. Cheater cider, but I add more spices," she said, picking up his term.

Annie almost forgot Mitch was standing there until he shifted his position, showing impatience. Too bad such an attractive man had such a surly disposition.

As the men stood side by side, she realized Cole and Mitch were nearly identical in height. She figured about six feet.

Annie had wished for more inches but had to be content with her sixty-four.

She opened the door and the men left.

Leaning against it, she stared at her tree and wondered again about Mitch's antagonism toward her. What had she done to merit that instant dislike? Pursing her lips, she banished thoughts of that unpleasant man and mulled over Cole.

Her first impression of him had been wrong. Well, maybe not totally, but wrong enough for her to want to know him better, along with the boys. *Know him better? What a silly thing to think. You downright enjoyed being around him.*

Right. And even when he'd touched a couple of personal points, he seemed to understand and back off. Not like a few of men she'd dated and pegged as "sensitive types." Men who wanted to probe her psyche even after she'd indicated a particular subject was off limits.

And darn it if Cole's smile didn't make her just a teeny bit weak in the knees.

She pushed that thought away. It was time to make the

cheater cider, add her special spices and go out and celebrate the season.

And, hopefully, Cole and his boys will stop by.

UNABLE TO SLEEP AND NOT INTERESTED IN WATCHING TV OR reading, Cole peeked through the blind in his bedroom, safe from detection by Annie because as usual he turned off most of the house lights once the boys were in bed. He realized about a year ago that he felt less alone in the dark.

However, Annie obviously loved lights. There was her outdoor display and several were still on in her house. Maybe she was still up writing or drawing. Hadn't she said she often wrote all night?

Cole dropped the blind, impatient and not liking the feeling.

Dinner had been uneasy as the boys were crabby, overtired from their snowshoeing expedition, and they went to bed shortly after barely finishing their chocolate ice cream. Tomorrow was a school day, the last week of school before Christmas break.

And thankfully Mitch left soon after that. He'd stared holes at Cole all during dinner. Just because he'd asked Annie over for dinner? How inane was that?

It was just a being-nice-to-a-neighbor gesture. *Right, then why did your pulse quicken with you caught her staring at you while you were touching one or another of her Christmas tree ornaments?*

Maybe he was impatient, edgy because he realized the

dreaded time for them to decorate their own Christmas tree was upon them. But maybe, just maybe, it wouldn't be quite as painful this year.

Since moving to Boulder, with new sights and a new home, away from things that were daily reminders of Lauren, Cole realized he wasn't always comparing every moment, every action to ones they'd shared. It was the beginning of the healing he'd been told would happen; he just hadn't believed the therapist and refused to go back for more sessions.

Along with the healing, his libido had been switched on for the first time in two years, and now was keeping him painfully awake.

The face attached to the yearning was Annie's.

She was definitely a fascinating mixture. First the she-cat, as she berated him about his role as a father—one he wasn't good at anyway. Then he glimpsed her other side: when she'd been all softness as she talked about her father, but then had gone all feisty again as she defended Josh about coming over to visit.

Cole wasn't a great father, not even a good one, which was why Mitch's daily help was a Godsend. But maybe Mitch was doing too much, and Cole way too little.

Oddly, it was the mighty mouse next door that was bringing him to that conclusion.

Nonetheless, it didn't change the fact that he had few skills at the job of being a parent and learning on the job was damned hard.

4

ANNIE SLIPPED ON HER COMFY BOSTON COLLEGE SWEATS and her well-worn sheepskin slippers and padded the few steps to her office, adjacent but completely separate from her bedroom. Turning on the computer, she waited as her daily calendar popped up on the screen.

"Yikes, how can it be Wednesday already," Annie said aloud, staring at the screen in total dismay. Two and a half weeks until Christmas, followed by two weeks until her deadline.

Although it was just past seven in the morning, and barely light outside, she'd hoped for a slow windup to the day after getting a rare eight hours of sleep. So much for that luxury.

Thankfully she wasn't nursing a headache any longer from the snowblower slip and fall, and the bump on the back her head was gone. Nevertheless, her deadline had suffered because she didn't feel like writing.

She'd never *not* felt like writing, and knew she had to

shake off that self-indulgence quickly. Her publisher had planned book tours and library readings for this book, and as a cherry on top, she had the launch of a new line of plush toys for three of her most popular star characters to look forward to.

Annie had never licensed her characters before, even though she'd been approached since making the NYT Best Seller list for children. However, this particular toy company made everything in America and she had final say on the design, so she jumped at the chance.

Despite the fact that her lifestyle was supplemented in a huge way by the income from the sizable estate her daddy had left her, writing and making sure she kept her fans and publisher happy, were her life's blood. A missed deadline wasn't going to happen, ever.

Shaking her head, she glanced away from the computer screen and looked out her office window to the house next door, its lights shining in the gray dawn of morning.

Sunday, after her chat and latte with Cole, when she'd specifically extended the invitation for cider, she stupidly hoped they'd drop by, but had subsequently been disappointed. Maybe she'd been too obvious. Or maybe Cole just didn't feel the same frisson of attraction for her that had zinged up her spine and settled in her belly as she'd watched him caress one, then another of the Christmas ornaments on her tree.

A blinking red light on her monitor pulled her attention away from Cole Evans, Josh and Peter.

The warning light Annie used for important reminders

was telling her that not only had she'd promised to create *and* read a short story at the Flatirons Elementary holiday program the end of next week, but also to make a star in the likeness of that book's character to go in the library case along with the book. It would be her third year of doing this and she loved it, but how in the heck had the deadline on that project snuck up on her?

You know why, your mind isn't in the game right now. Damn Cole Evans's sapphire blue eyes and his peppermint lattes.

Annie forced her attention to the other flashing calendar note.

Jenny was coming over for dinner tonight.

Annie needed coffee before she could get a grip on planning her day.

Just then the doorbell rang. Who would be coming around before the sun was fully up? Only Jenny would do that to her, but then she had a key and wouldn't have bothered ringing the bell. Annie ran down the stairs and flung open the door.

To find Cole wearing a sheepish look.

"Oh, it's you."

"I'm wounded."

Annie laughed out loud, enjoying his sense of humor that matched her own, a bit sarcastic and a bit flippant. "I thought maybe Jenny was in some sort of trouble."

"Jenny?"

"My best friend, you'll meet her someday." She looked closely at him. He hadn't shaved, and was wearing sweats.

OMG, so was she. Baggy, wonderfully comfy sweats on

a cold frosty morning. Oh well, it didn't matter anyway—she wasn't on the prowl for Cole Evans. *Liar.*

"What brings you over? Is one of the boys sick? Did you need something," she asked, words rushing over themselves as she realized the truth of her words. Cole Evans was worth dressing up for.

"May I come in?" he asked as his breath blew out in white frosty puffs.

"Of course." She stepped back to allow him room to enter, closed the door and waited for him to tell her what brought him to her house this early.

"We ran out of milk. I was going to feed the boys toast and peanut butter instead of their favorite cereal, but Josh suggested he run over and ask if you could spare some. He wouldn't let it drop, so here I am."

Annie laughed again. It felt like such an out-of-character thing for him to do.

"You should have sent him over. I don't bite, you know."

"Yes, but he'd want to hang around and mornings are hectic enough without him being pokey."

"You are going to let him come over someday, aren't you? Really, I'm safe and even fun to be around."

The smile that creased his cheeks and crinkled his eyes once again left her breathless. "Of course I'm going to let him come by. Just remember I warned you."

"I'll cry for help if I need it," Annie said, returning his smile, standing there drinking in all the sexiness of it.

"The milk?" Cole asked, his smile growing, if possible, even wider.

"Ah yes. I went to the market yesterday and bought a

gallon, but it's fat-free," she said quickly trying to cover her blatant reaction to the man in front of her.

"We're used to fat-free. Can I borrow a couple of cups?"

"Follow me." Annie led the way into her kitchen, turning back to see Cole slow down and stare as he entered the room.

"Wow, this is incredible. Do you like to cook, or are you a chef in your spare time?"

"I love to cook—it's a stress reliever for me. I just finished the last of the remodeling this summer."

"You did all this yourself?"

"God no. I meant the contractors finished. I'm kinda picky so it took a while to make all the decisions." She looked around the open, airy kitchen with pride.

The dark cherry cabinets were handle-free, a simple push and they sprang open. The stainless-steel appliances were gourmet quality and the sand-colored, maroon flecked granite made the kitchen feel warm and inviting. Glass-fronted cabinets held her collection of crystal.

Annie loved drinking out of crystal—it made her feel elegant and as if she'd gone back in time when using fine stemware was de rigueur.

"Well, I'm impressed. I hate to cook, but regardless I have to redo my kitchen soon. I knew it when I bought the place."

"I'm pretty sure old man Thompson still used an ice box."

"Not that bad, but close."

"I'll help with the design if you want."

The minute the words left her lips, she cringed. Always

being the helpful one. She sighed, waiting for the gleam in his eyes to dull and the icy distance of their first meeting to return.

"It's a deal."

Annie grinned as she pulled the milk carton out of the fridge. "Here, take the whole thing. I'm going out today—I'll grab another."

"Mitch or I will be going to the market later, so I'll replace this today. You're a lifesaver."

"My pleasure. Say hi to Josh and Peter for me."

Annie opened the front door and Cole left, sprinting the short distance to his house.

Smiling again, she gently closed the huge wooden door, then went back to the kitchen and pushed the button on her coffee machine. As the dark aroma of coffee filled the air, she sat at the granite counter, chin resting her on fingers, staring into space, and realized Cole Evans had turned from vampire to a man who was beginning to enthrall her thoughts. *Isn't that what vampires do? Enthrall their victims?*

The coffee machine finished its job, and she pulled the cup from beneath the spout and headed back to her office, wondering if her next book should have a vampire *and* a star in it. Would vampires scare the youngest of her audience?

COLE HAD TO HURRY THE BOYS THROUGH BREAKFAST WHILE he fixed peanut butter sandwiches—strawberry jelly for

Peter and honey for Josh—filled baggies with carrots and celery, others with brownies, and tucked in money for milk.

Milk.

How could such a simple thing as borrowing milk keep flashing in his mind?

Because the woman you borrowed it from looked sleepy and warm in her sweats, like she'd just risen from bed.

And that image, coupled with his newly reawakened sexual desire, gave Cole all too vivid images of him and Annie, entwined, skin to skin...

He shook the image away, knowing that sex for sex's sake wasn't his style. And since he wasn't about to get involved with anyone anytime soon, it meant that any relationship with Annie wasn't going to happen.

Dealing with backpacks and bundling the boys into his Honda Pilot pulled his thoughts from the woman next door.

He headed for Flatirons Elementary School. Not a long drive, five minutes or less, but once there, the queue for dropping off kids was a much longer wait.

The boys in the backseat were talking about the scores they got last night on Angry Birds, and Cole tuned them out as his thoughts turned again to his neighbor.

Josh had asked every day to visit next door, and either Cole or Mitch had found some reason for him not to go.

Now Cole had no more excuses, nor did he want to find them. Mitch however, never seemed to run out of them. His brother-in-law didn't like Annie one bit, and at first Cole was sure Mitch had Annie pegged right; a meddling neighbor who was lonely and maybe love starved and would latch onto Cole at the first opportunity.

However Cole was pretty sure Annie was anything but love starved. She was too pretty and too saucy not to have men after her in droves.

Since most of his neighbors seemed to think highly of Annie and would do anything to help her as she helped them, he doubted she was lonely.

"Better not let Sammy see that brownie at lunch, or you'll have to give it to him."

"Will not, he'll have to take it from me."

Cole braked suddenly. "What are you two talking about?"

"Sammy's in Peter's class—"

"Let Peter tell me, please." Cole turned in his seat to stare at his oldest son. "Are you having trouble with a classmate?"

Peter glared at Josh.

"Peter?"

"Sammy isn't a problem. I can handle him."

"I don't want you handling him. Where did you get the idea you should be doing that?"

Peter looked uncomfortable, then instantly defensive. "Uncle Mitch. He said we need to stand up for ourselves at all times."

The car behind Cole's honked and he irritably waved it around him.

"Dad, it's not a big thing. And Uncle Mitch is taking us to karate lessons after Christmas so we can learn how to protect ourselves the right way."

"We're going to a Dojohn," Josh chimed in.

"Dojo, nitwit."

"Don't call your brother names," Cole corrected automatically.

A bell rang loudly, signaling an end to this conversation for now as the boys jumped out of the car, slammed the doors and ran into the low, single-story school building with the last of the straggling students. Cole hadn't even had the chance to say goodbye.

Feeling once again like a pretty dismal father figure, he drove home to shower, shave and get the day going.

Additionally, after what he'd just heard, he needed to talk to Mitch, who hadn't run the idea past him about the boys taking karate lessons. He wasn't against it but realized with a new burst of shame that Mitch was making decisions he shouldn't be making. Taking on too much responsibility that he didn't need to take on. That Cole had allowed him to assume.

Shaved and showered, he ran down the stairs. After leaving a message on Mitch's phone that they needed to talk, Cole headed out. The streets were wet with melting snow runoff and slush. Driving down Broadway to Table Mesa and up toward the mesa and NCAR, Cole mentally noted to stop at the market on the way back home. He owed Annie a jug of milk. *Perfect excuse to see her again.*

He groaned aloud, surprising himself with the sound. Maybe it would be better to see if Mitch could pick it up and Josh could take it over to Annie. That way he'd make two people happy. Josh, who kept nagging him about Annie's invitation, and himself, so he wouldn't have to deal with Annie's subtle sexy appeal. Allure that switched on hormones he hadn't experienced since Lauren became sick.

Walking into his office, he was immediately besieged by his engineer about their latest particulate measuring instrument that was running too hot and skewing the data.

The day fled and it was dark by the time Cole walked into his house.

Josh was pouting at the kitchen table, sending glares toward Mitch.

What now?

"Daddy, Uncle Mitch says I can't take over the milk we owe to Annie."

Cole quirked a brow at Mitch.

"I said I'd drop it off after I left here. I'm sure Annie isn't waiting on pins and needles for it. Besides it's dark outside," Mitch said, a trace of irritation coloring his voice.

"And I told you Dad promised I could take it over, and I wanted to go since before it got dark," Josh countered.

"I *did* say you could, so why did you wait until now?"

Josh gave him an unbelieving look. "Because," he drew out the word in the way only a child could, "Uncle Mitch wouldn't *let* me."

Irritation quickly snaked up Cole's back. "Go on now, and I'll watch from the door to make sure you're okay. Don't stay too long. Dinner will be ready in about..." he looked at Mitch.

"Thirty minutes, and call when you're ready to come home—I'll watch for you," Mitch said.

I'll watch for you? Had Cole created an artificial father

figure the boys paid more attention to than they did their real father? Or was it worry over Annie that set Mitch off and emboldened his control over the boys?

"HEY, JOSH, COME IN." ANNIE WELCOMED THE BOY INTO HER house. "Perfect timing, I was getting ready to make mashed potatoes and remembered I didn't have the milk. So I was going to punt and use half and half."

She took the carton from Josh and led the way into the kitchen.

"You were going to punt a ball in your kitchen? Mom would never let us do that."

Annie smiled as he looked around. It was a big room, but not big enough for that. "Sorry, kiddo, it's an expression; go with what you've got. No football in this kitchen either."

Josh grinned at her.

"Can you stay for a while?"

"Yeah."

"Had dinner yet?"

"Nope."

"Darn, I baked muffins today, but they'll spoil your dinner. I'll give you two, one for you and one for Peter for lunch tomorrow."

Annie drained the pot of chunked potatoes and got out her mixer. Putting in butter, milk and sour cream she whipped the potatoes and gave Josh a spoonful to try. "What do you think? More salt?"

She waited as he carefully tasted half the spoonful, then the last of it and deliberated as if this was the most crucial question in the world at the moment.

"Perfect. Can I have some more?"

Fixing him a small bowl, she added another tiny pat of butter and handed it to him.

"Can I see where you write?" he asked, the words muffled around a mouthful of potatoes.

Annie glanced at him as she covered the pot and set it on the warmer burner.

"The roast isn't ready yet, and Jenny's late as usual. I'd love to show you. Sure you've got time?"

"Yeah."

Annie led the way upstairs to her office, let Josh go in first and turned on the lights.

Josh looked like he was in Disneyland. His eyes widened, filled with the excitement of actually seeing the characters he knew and loved up close and personal. "That's Kamen and look, that's Little Bear, right?"

"Right," Annie said, watching him closely.

"Little Bear helped Oscar when he lost his mother," Josh said.

"You're right, and do you remember what Little Bear did to help Oscar?"

"He found a star for Oscar to look at and name for his mother."

"Have you looked for a star to name after your mother? Then you'll know where you can look when you miss her."

"No." Josh kicked at the thick rug covering part of the oak floor. "Annie, why did you pick stars to help kids?"

This was a question Annie got all the time, usually from children a bit older, and it pleased her that Josh would think about it. "Stars are where we came from. They're made up of all the elements we have in our bodies. They were here first, then us, so it seemed natural that they would guide us, like they guided the sailors long ago, or the ancient astronomers. We all have stardust inside us."

Josh nodded wisely.

Annie smiled. "Do you understand?"

"Kinda."

"And that's okay for now, just as long as you believe that Little Bear and Kamen and all the others are helping those they choose to help."

"You have to believe, right? To have them choose you?"

Oh, this was tricky ground. She wanted the children she wrote for to believe that her characters helped the children they chose, and thus maybe help them cope with whatever crisis they were facing, but not think the stars would really come to life for them.

But then kids believed in Santa, so she felt relatively safe in agreeing with Josh. "Yes, you have to believe when you make a wish. Did you know one of my favorite stars is right here in Boulder, only visible at Christmas time?"

"Where?"

"The Flagstaff star, right above our houses, up on the mountain. Close enough to touch. Manmade, of course, but so beautiful."

The doorbell pealed. "That's got to be Jenny, I'll introduce you. You'll like her."

They went downstairs and Annie pulled open the door, only to find Cole whose brow was deeply furrowed.

Uh-oh.

She swiveled to look at Josh, who looked guilty.

Okay. What was up?

"Hey, Cole, come in. Josh and I were up in my office—"

"Yeah, she's got a cool desk to draw on and all cool stuff and a computer that can read back her writing to her and—"

"That's great Josh. Tell me over dinner okay? You're late, big time."

"Aw, Dad, it's just spaghetti. And Annie has muffins for Peter and me."

Just then Jenny pulled up in the driveway.

"Wow, something smells delicious," Jen said as she approached the open front door and extended her hand to Cole, smiling at Josh. "Hi, Jennifer Malone. You must be the next-door neighbor, Dr. Evans."

"Call me Cole," he said, shooting a swift glance at Annie, who caught it but chose to ignore it. She did, however, notice that he took Jenny's hand and held it a moment longer than the handshake. Well, Jenny had that effect on everybody. Men found her beautiful, women enjoyed her company, and kids weren't afraid of her.

Jen bent to hold her hand out to Josh. "And you're Josh, right?"

"Yeah, how'd you know?" He said, taking her hand and politely shaking it.

"Annie told me that she had a fan living next door, and I figured it wasn't your father."

Annie widened her eyes; the subtext of her friend's comment wasn't lost on her, nor apparently Cole.

"Oh, I'm growing to be a fan of Annabelle Hamilton. Come on, Josh, Uncle Mitch is waiting for us."

"Annie, will you make your potatoes for us someday? And what about the muffins?"

Annie looked at Cole and saw the smile on his lips echo in his eyes. Making him again look human and approachable, and damn him, desirable.

Heat flowed through her, her cheeks grew warm and the world receded.

Annie couldn't blink, didn't want to. What she really wanted was his lips on hers, his body pressed against her, hard.

"Annie? Will you?"

Breaking the magnetism of his gaze, she glanced at Jen to find that knowing look in her eyes. She quickly shifted her gaze to Josh, who was earnestly waiting for her answer.

"Potatoes. Ah yes. Anytime, Josh, and pot roast. They're one of my favorite winter meals to make. And I'll save you some muffins. Promise."

"Cool. Dad, her mashed potatoes taste great."

Cole gently grasped his son by the shoulder and pointed him toward home.

"I meant it about dinner. Just give me a few hours warning," she called after them. Then stood back, biting her lip. What on earth possessed her to do that?

Duh, it was his "Oh, I'm growing to be a fan of Annabelle Hamilton," *and those fine blue eyes.*

Jen turned her around, pushed her back into the

house, closed the door, marched her into the kitchen and poured two glasses of Cabernet, all without saying a word.

"So that was the vampire? He can bite me anytime."

Annie stared at her friend, then burst out laughing. "You are incorrigible."

"And like I said Saturday night at your lighting event, you're headed for trouble."

Already there, my friend, already there.

5

"So now please give our own star, Annabelle Hamilton, a big welcome," the principal of Flatirons Elementary, Sally Lefferdink announced.

Annie stood from her seat in the front row, amazed at the exuberant applause from the kids, and she hadn't even announced her special treat. The boxes had just been delivered to the school and the gifts were waiting to be handed out.

As she scanned the back of the room for a special familiar face, she realized there were more parents standing there than the last two years.

She paused when she reached Cole and darn it all, Mitch.

"Annie, here, over here."

She looked to see Josh standing and waving at her. Grinning, she waved back, and the smile splitting his face as he sat down told her she'd made his day. It was wonderful to have such an ardent fan.

Glancing at the teachers, their arms full of her newly printed and bound *Star Light, Star Bright* story, especially written for the students at Flatirons, she nodded and they passed out the books.

She sat on the stool in front of the group. "You can read along with me if you want or just listen. This is my holiday treat for you, and only you guys."

Twenty minutes later, the room was silent except for a book closing here or there as Annie closed her own book. "I hope you enjoyed hearing Jeffrey's story and meeting Maximus, my new star."

Reaching into the satchel she'd brought along with her, she handed Principal Lefferdink the carving she'd created that looked like Maximus.

"This will go in our Annabelle case. Thank you for this wonderful honor you've given Flatirons Elementary School."

Lunch recess began and Annie stayed chatting with some of the faculty and autographing books for the kids that asked.

Josh came toward her, flanked by his father. Annie quickly scanned the auditorium to find Mitch leaning against the wall, arms crossed, watching them.

He was too far away for her to see his expression clearly, but the crossed arms told her enough. Why did he dislike her so much? She wasn't trying to be anything more than a friend to the boys. But he seemed almost obsessed with caring for them. And Cole seemed to allow that—something she didn't understand. But she clearly understood that Mitch needed a family of his own. Kids and a wife to dote on.

Then the nearness of Cole pushed everything else out of her mind.

She hadn't been face to face with him for over a week, and God help her, she'd missed him. *Silly girl*, she chastised herself. *If you're not careful you'll start acting like a love-sick teenager.*

Start? She was already there.

During the past few days, Annie had hovered next to a window to watch for him when she knew it near time for him to bundle the boys into his Pilot for school, and even worse, she'd rush to her office window when she heard him pull into his driveway at night.

A couple of times Annie had seen Cole pause to stare at her house, maybe trying to figure out which room she could be in. She'd quickly pulled back from the window, knowing she'd rather be tarred and feathered than have him see her spying on him.

Feeling heat bloom in her cheeks as if indeed she'd just been caught, she took a deep breath when Josh reached her and turned her attention wholly on him.

"Annie, please sign my book, and be sure to write 'To Josh' on it, okay?"

"Okay, kiddo. Did you like the story?"

He nodded vigorously. "Especially when Maximus showed Jeffrey how to get home."

"Have you learned yet that long, long ago, sailors used the stars to navigate, to find the right direction to sail toward their destination? And then used the stars to navigate back home again?"

Josh shook his head. "So stars really do help us?"

"Yep, and not just sailors. When you learn some of the constellations, you can find your way by following them. Like the North Star in the constellation Ursa Minor.

"Cool, I want to be a star follower."

"An astronomer?"

His brow wrinkled at the word.

"Someone who studies stars," she clarified, and handed him his book back, signed as requested.

He opened the book. "To my good friend and fan, Josh Evans. May you always follow the stars and find the path they'll lead you toward," he read aloud.

"Thanks, Annie," he yelled as he ran off, waving his book to his buddies as they raced outside for recess.

"It's a nice gesture to give all the kids their own copy of the story," Cole said.

"Maybe in a hundred years, it'll be worth something on the Antiques Roadshow," she said with a smile.

"Then I'll be sure to put Josh and Peter's copy in the vault. No more reading this book for them."

"You might have a fight on your hands with Josh. How about if I give you your very own autographed copy?"

"That would be nice. And you're right about Josh—he'll never give up that copy now. Listen, I'm headed downtown to try out Pizzeria Locale. Want to join me?"

Annie couldn't help it, she immediately looked to the spot where Mitch stood, only to find him not there.

"Is Mitch coming?"

"No, he has a meeting with a potential client for a huge web project."

"He's a web designer?"

"One of the best around. He has clever ideas and is building a great business with his talent."

"So that's how he can be so available for the boys?"

"Yep."

His "yep" sounded a bit hesitant, as if things weren't going smoothly at the Evans household. Was that her fault for mentioning that Mitch seemed to be taking over what should be Cole's role?

Maybe she should learn to keep her mouth shut. But she wasn't going to lose this opportunity to have some alone time with Cole. "I'd love to go to lunch, actually. I've wanted to go there myself, so this is perfect. Let me put the school's book and Maximus in their new home, and we can go."

They headed down the hall to the open glass case, set into the wall between Principal Lefferdink's office and the library, when a little girl, probably a third grader came running into the office. "They're fighting near the jungle-gym—I'm scared."

Principal Lefferdink, Cole and the school's secretary ran out to the playground. Annie stuffed her book and Maximus into the case and ran after them.

~

"WHAT THE HELL?" COLE STOPPED ONLY FOR AN INSTANT AS Peter and another boy were rolling on the ground, fists pummeling each other, mud and snow flying.

"Sammy, stop it," Josh shouted, trying to push the boy off Peter.

Then Peter screamed and blood gushed from his nose.

"Josh, move away," Cole instructed his son, as he pulled the boy called Sammy off Peter. But not fast enough as Sammy got in one more kick, connecting with Peter's arm, and he screamed again.

Principal Lefferdink waded into the fray, taking Sammy from Cole, keeping a tight grip on the squirming boy.

"Call 911," Cole yelled as he cradled his bleeding son.

"Ow. My arm, Dad. It really hurts."

"Paramedics are on their way," the principal told Cole, then turned to suggest the other teachers shepherd the stunned kids off the playground back into school and, with Sammy firmly in tow, headed back into the building herself.

"Sammy started it," Josh said, tears beginning to fall. "Will Peter be okay?"

Cole begged Annie with his gaze, hoping she'd understand, grateful when she kneeled and put an arm around Josh.

"He'll be fine, honey. I think he'll have to go the emergency room, but we'll go with him because he'll need us there. Are you okay with that?" she asked calmly, but with a confidence Cole knew Josh would respond well to.

"Are you coming?"

"You bet."

"Dad, I'm afraid," Peter said.

It took Cole a second to realize Peter wasn't afraid of his arm being broken, he was afraid of being in the hospital.

"Petey-boy, we won't be in there long. This will be a simple fix, I promise," Cole said, using the nickname Lauren gave their elder son.

"But Mom—"

"Mom was sick. You're hurt. It's different, I promise."

"Peter, did you know my dad was a doctor?" Annie asked him. "We lived in Maine. Dad was the only doc around for several towns. I can't tell you how many times he fixed up broken arms and dislocated shoulders, and everyone was always right as rain."

"Right as rain?"

"A saying that means everything turns out okay."

Annie was taking Peter's mind off what loomed before him, and Cole was appreciative of the distraction she gave him.

Cole also noticed that Josh was leaning hard into Annie's embrace.

"Dad, Sammy called me a baby," Josh said, tears in his voice.

"Sammy said Josh still wore diapers if he liked those silly books, so I pushed him. He pushed back and I fell down," Peter said.

"Then Sammy started punching him," Josh said.

Cole met Annie's gaze. He'd thought he'd see disapproval in it, but all he saw was compassion and worry.

"We'll work this out later," Cole said gently to Josh. "Let's get Petey-boy all patched up and then we'll talk."

Sirens sounded and though it felt like an eon, Cole knew it had only been minutes between the principal's phone call and the paramedics now arriving at their side.

In another few minutes Peter was on a gurney being loaded into the back of the ambulance.

Cole climbed in to be beside him on the trip, thankful that Annie had Josh with her and was following them to the hospital.

WHILE PETER WAS IN X-RAY, ANNIE AND JOSH WENT TO THE hospital cafeteria to get coffee for the adults and hot chocolate for Josh.

Cole was left alone in the small curtained cubicle, inside a place he hated with a passion.

Images of Lauren's last breath played in his mind. A scenario he'd refused to relive … until now. A tear tickled his cheek, and he didn't bother to wipe it away.

One tear, then hundreds fell, soaking his shirt and he made no effort to stem the tide.

He'd only gone to one counseling session after her death and hadn't realized just how lonely a path he'd embarked upon by going it alone. The boys needed comforting, Mitch needed comforting, and he'd given them his all, but he hadn't looked for any himself.

And who could he have found comfort with?

His colleagues? He didn't even give that a second thought. Mitch?

He and Mitch didn't talk, at least not in the sense of being confidants, not since he and Lauren got married. It had changed their relationship, which was only natural.

Cole sat on the hard plastic chair, feeling the ever-present and heavy weight of loss begin to lift as years of tears flowed.

He didn't want to forget Lauren; she would forever be a part of him, but he did desperately want to move on with life.

And he knew Annie could have a part in his moving forward.

Mopping his face with his handkerchief, knowing there was nothing he could do about his soaked shirt, he took several deep breaths to regain composure. Annie and Josh would be returning soon, and he didn't need to scare Josh any more than he already was.

Sure enough a couple minutes later, Cole heard his name called from the other side of the stiff beige curtain.

"In here, still waiting for Peter to get back from X-ray," he said, getting up from the chair and pulling aside the drape.

Seeing the cardboard tray in her hands filled with three cups took him back to Sunday over a week ago when he brought Annie coffee to her house.

She shared his slight smile. "Yeah, but these are not peppermint lattes."

"Scary if you're going to always read my mind."

He followed her gaze as it swept his face and took in his soaked shirt.

Bless her for not saying anything about it or asking why.

"Dad, I got whipped cream on my cocoa."

Cole focused on his younger son, as if seeing him clearly after a fog lifted. "Hey, that's my favorite way to drink it, too."

"Really?" Josh lit up. "I didn't know that. Can we have some at home?"

Was it really that simple to make Josh happy? Sharing a cup of hot cocoa and whipped cream? *No, you know it's not, but it is a good moment to share with my boys.*

The ER doc came into the cubicle. "Dr. Evans, Peter has a metaphyseal fracture of the radial bone in his arm. It's what I expected after you said he was kicked."

Black grimness invaded Cole. How dare his son suffer the pain and subsequent healing because another child bullied him?

"So, first I need to splint it until the swelling goes down, then four to six weeks in a cast, then about a month to strengthen the bone before he's fit to do much of anything," the doc said. "No jungle gyms, tumbling or such activities. He's going to need sedation for me to put the bones back in place, and he's asking for you to be with him."

Cole looked at Annie, who again seemed to read his thoughts.

"If it's okay with you—and Josh of course—I thought

I'd take Josh home with me. Once Peter is settled, we'll head to your house."

"Josh? Want to go with Annie?"

"Sure, but you'll be here without us."

Cole gathered Josh close and whispered in his ear. "I'll be fine. And, Josh Petosh, I love you with all my heart."

He kissed him on the cheek, watched Annie take his hand as he carefully clutched the cup of hot cocoa with whipped cream in the other and left the hospital.

Cole followed the ER doc to the surgery suite and held Peter's unhurt hand in his.

"Dad, he said I was going to get sleepy. I'll wake up, right?"

"Yep, then we'll head home. Are you ready?"

At Peter's nod, the IV started.

Knowing sedation and the setting of his bone was necessary to help Peter didn't alleviate the alarm filling him as Peter grew drowsy and his eyes closed.

"I'm here, son. I'm right here," Cole whispered into his ear.

6

WHAT A DAY.

Going from the high of reading her book to an attentive audience at Flatirons Elementary to the fear of being helpless while Peter was in the doctor's hands, Annie couldn't wait for the clock to tick toward midnight and a new day to begin.

Josh was asleep on an air mattress on the floor in her studio, with a sample of her new plush star Alpha tucked in beside him.

Her "real" guest room was downstairs, at the back of her house, private and quiet, but she didn't want Josh to be that far away from her.

The little boy had tried to stay awake, but nature took over, and soon his eyes were half mast, then closed, his brown, impossibly long lashes resting against his cheeks.

As Annie bent over and kissed his forehead, a deep, keen yearning filled her.

She wanted her own children. To kiss them goodnight and wish them sweet dreams.

An impossible reality.

Annie had thought of adopting, but in a moment of insight she admitted to herself that she also wanted the whole ticket. A family *and* a husband to share her life with.

Her dad had been a single parent, not by his choice, but by the choice her mother made. Living the small town life in Maine had stifled her and she left.

Annie thought she'd see her mother again someday, but it hadn't happened and actually life had been less stressful without her.

Daddy had made it clear in a thousand little actions that Annie was always the most important person in his life. They'd had a great time. Not a conventional upbringing, but wonderful and exciting, and she had more responsibility given to her than any other child her age.

So maybe it was time to change her thinking and become a single parent herself and not depend on finding a man. She could give her child as much love as her dad had given her.

Glancing down at Josh again, Annie gently ran a finger down his cheek and left, keeping the door ajar.

Leaving the hall light on in case Josh woke and didn't realize where he was, she moved to her bedroom, knelt on the window seat and watched for lights to go on in Cole's house.

Josh was worried about Peter, and she didn't blame him; she was a bit frantic herself. She knew the arm splinting wasn't hard, but Peter was already afraid of the hospital and that had something to do with his mom's illness.

Annie didn't try to stifle her sigh. She couldn't forget that Cole was a widower, and while he'd been nicer, even joking with her, it didn't mean anything more than being neighborly. Not a lover. Just a friend.

And isn't that what she wanted too?

She was smart enough to realize she had physical needs and wanted a healthy sex life, but she wouldn't put herself in the position of being rejected again for something that had been completely out of her control. Anything more than being friends and lovers was out of the picture.

Finally seeing Cole's Honda Pilot pull into his driveway, followed by Mitch's Jeep, she watched as the two men helped a very woozy Peter out of the car and into the house.

Annie quietly went downstairs to wait.

Ten long minutes later, she heard the knock and hoped it was Cole, not Mitch coming to get Josh.

Indeed, a weary and stressed Cole stood there.

"Come in, is everything okay? You look exhausted. How is Peter?"

"Peter's fine. Well, as fine as can be expected. Mitch is with him until he falls asleep—which should be in about five minutes—so I could come over and retrieve Josh."

"He's asleep, fell asleep watching Star Wars. Would you like to leave him here for the night? I can bring him over when he wakes up. I'm a light sleeper, I'll hear him."

"I hate to wake him, but that seems like one more imposition I'm putting on you."

"Cole, you should know by now that Josh is very special to me. None of this has been, as you put it, an imposition. Being there for you, Josh and Peter has been a pleasure. Well not a pleasure—heck, you know what I mean."

"We're lucky to have moved next door."

Annie felt the heat of his gaze all the way to her toes. "You didn't think that two weeks ago," she said.

"No? Then I was wrong," he said, in a voice sounding like smooth cognac, all traces of exhaustion gone.

Going to her head just like the liquor. Burning a path all the way to the tips of her toes.

She fought the weakness in her knees and the flutter in her belly. Hadn't she just decided that Cole was best as a friend?

He reached toward her, tucking a stray lock of hair behind her ear.

Annie turned her face to nestle in his palm.

His other hand cupped her cheek and he stepped closer, raising her face to his.

He brushed her lips once, as if testing her.

She snaked her arms around his neck pulling him closer as her answer.

His lips settled over hers, warm, soft, then hard and teasing. Then his hands moved from her face to her back, bringing their bodies together.

Heady with the potency of his kiss, she melted forward,

feeling his lean and toned body under her searching hands, ruing the fabric that separated them.

Cole was someone who could easily get under her defenses, and she wasn't about to let them all down at the first kiss.

She pulled back enough to break contact, regretting the instant she moved.

Running a finger down his cheek and gently touching his lips, Annie wanted to make sure Cole knew she wasn't sorry for this moment between them.

He looked at her with hooded eyes, heavy with the same desire she was doing her best to tamp down.

"What if I told you this isn't over?" he whispered in her ear.

Hot, liquid yearning flooded her at the promise in his voice.

"I would tell you back that I'm pleased."

"Pleased? Annie, you don't know pleased."

"Is that so, Cole Evans, PhD?" she said, an impish smile on her lips. "I guess I'll just have to find out for myself."

He moved to take her back into his arms, she took one step back. "But let's take it slow, okay?"

He stood hands on his hips, looking almost exasperated. Then shook his head. "Okay. Back to neutral ground."

"Oh, I think we're a bit past neutral."

Finally his grin emerged. "Deal. Peter isn't going to school tomorrow, and neither is Josh, which is fine as Christmas break starts next week. I have to meet with

Principal Lefferdink tomorrow and see what I have to tackle regarding the fight."

"What time should I get Josh up?"

Cole pulled his phone from his pocket and glanced at it. "God, it's one a.m. How about letting him sleep in. That is, if that's okay with you?"

"It's fine, more than fine. Don't worry, he's safe here."

"I know and I'm grateful."

Annie touched Cole's arm as he was about to leave. "I'm so sorry this happened."

"What, the kiss?"

"No, silly. Peter getting hurt in a fight."

"Me too."

Quickly he bent and brushed her lips again, then, without a word, slipped through the door.

Her Christmas lights were on, so she was able to see him until he moved past her carport. She touched her lips, wondering what made Cole kiss her. She didn't think it was merely a thank you kiss.

No, it had far more passion behind it than a simple thanks.

And suddenly, with that kiss, everything changed. But was it for the better, or was it induced by the stress and this was its subsequent relief?

ANNIE FELT SOMEONE POKING HER SHOULDER JUST AS HER alarm sounded with "Where Are You Christmas" from the

Grinch. The song was a gentle way to wake up during this holiday season.

"Annie, is Peter okay?"

"Hey, sweetie, good morning." She yawned and patted the bed. Josh climbed up, still holding his Alpha star and snuggled next to her.

"Peter got home really late last night, but your dad says he's fine. He's not going to school today, and neither are you."

"Yay. Can I come back here?"

"Maybe, it depends on your dad. I'm thinking he's going to have a lot to do with the school today, so bugging him about coming over might not be such a good idea. Do you understand?" She had no idea what the protocol was for that kind of physical altercation during school, but she was pretty sure it wasn't going to be an easy day for Cole.

At Josh's pout, Annie tucked a finger under his chin and raised it just a bit. "We'll have more time together, but it's kind of a hard moment for your dad, and I bet Peter would like to have you with him. Maybe you can let him win a few video games."

Josh's eyes lit up. "Yeah, I can do that. He'd like that. I play some games better than him."

"Ready to go home?"

"Yeah."

It was still dark outside, but her Christmas lights were still on and she walked hand in hand with Josh the short distance to his house. It was bitterly cold and snow was promised for the weekend.

Annie knocked lightly on Cole's door.

Mitch answered, and sharp disappointed flooded her.

"Good morning, Josh. Let's go up and get you bathed and dressed, then breakfast, okay?"

"Can I see Peter?"

"He's asleep."

"But I want to see him."

"That was the first question out of his mouth this morning, if Peter was okay," Annie interjected, worried that Mitch might not let Josh see for himself that Peter was home and safe.

"Of course he's okay," Mitch said.

"Annie told me he was, but I want to see."

Mitch looked at Annie, and she couldn't quite tell what was going on behind those shuttered eyes.

"Okay, Josh, you're home safe. I'll see you later." She wanted to hug Josh, but Mitch moved forward and made that impossible unless she pushed him aside.

Turning to head back to her home, a hug suddenly held her still. Looking down into Josh's upturned face, Annie bent down and kissed his cheek. The hell with Mitch standing there.

"Bye, Annie, thanks for letting me keep Alpha."

"He has a good home with you."

She didn't deign to look at Mitch again and walked down the sidewalk, feeling his gaze bore holes into her back.

That man needed some serious counseling.

ANNIE OPENED ONE HEAVY EYELID TO GLANCE AT HER CLOCK. It was only six thirty on Sunday morning and as much as coffee beckoned, she didn't want to wake Jen, who'd had the last half of the second bottle of pinot grigio all by herself.

Last night, her best buddy had dropped by unannounced, as was often the case, bearing bottles of wine and "heavy" hors d'oeuvres. And when the snow ,which had threatened all day, started to fall, Jen decided on the wise course of staying put.

She kept spare clothes in the guest bedroom, makeup and toiletries in the attached bathroom, because she and Annie would often talk the night through. It was easier for Jen just to crawl into bed in the guest room instead of driving home clear across town to catch a few hours of sleep before heading off to her high-tech lab. Being one of the world's top digital forensic detectives paid quite well, even if it didn't give her much of a steady social life.

So instead of plodding downstairs and making the coffee she so craved, Annie pulled her feather duvet from the bed, threw it around her shoulders and curled up on her window seat to watch the snow fall, glittering in her Christmas lights. It was the kind of morning to stay in, and the Evans clan was doing exactly that as the house next door remained dark.

She hadn't heard from anyone over there since she'd dropped off Josh early Friday morning.

Deeply disappointed that Cole hadn't at least stopped by and told her how Peter fared, she figured something had scared him off.

Was it the kiss?

No, after all, he'd said, *What if I told you this isn't over?"*

Silly goose, you're the one who said take it slow.

"And don't forget he's the one that said, *so we're back to neutral ground*, even if you disputed it," Annie muttered to herself.

"Who said neutral?" Jenny said, entering the bedroom, bearing steaming mugs of coffee and her own duvet, wrapped around her shoulders.

Annie smiled as she took the mug from her bestest buddy. Whenever Jenny stayed over it was like a sleepover from their youth. Stories, wine—well, they hadn't had wine in those days, but makeup and food and chat.

A bit different now they were grown women... oh, who was she kidding, it was no different, just the drinks and the topic of conversation had changed.

But then, maybe not. Boys were big then and now.

"Spill it, Hamilton, who said neutral?"

"Cole did," Annie admitted, looking over the rim of her mug.

"And why would that particular word need to come up in a topic of conversation? He was what, talking about Switzerland?"

"You're a riot, you know that?" Annie said, knowing she'd have to come clean. "I said that we needed to take it slow, and he said, okay, back to neutral, and I said—"

"Just wait one second, why did you say you needed to take what slow?"

Annie sighed. "Going to make me confess the whole thing, right?"

"Darn tootin'."

Annie couldn't keep the sheepish look off her face.

"Don't tell me you slept with him."

"Not yet."

That earned her a second of surprised silence from her friend.

"What happened to the vampire and being East Coast and stuck up and—"

"I don't know. My first impression of him was flawed? I need my head examined?"

"So what did he do?"

"Kissed me." Annie tried to look nonchalant as she said the two words, but from the corner of her eye, she saw Jenny look toward the darkened house and then back at her, brows raised.

"And you're twitter-pated over a kiss? Annie child, you got it bad."

"Afraid so. It was all the peppermint latte's fault."

Jenny stared at her, then let loose her signature laugh, full bodied and low.

Annie knew men found her friend's laugh incredibly sexy, and most of them tried too hard to make it happen—unsuccessfully. Jenny had little time to date and was usually disappointed in the men she'd found.

Jen was incredibly smart and secure in herself and what she did. Men who weren't just couldn't keep up.

Annie's thoughts moved back to Cole. He seemed very secure in his own skin.

What she didn't understand was why he was apparently using his brother-in-law as a quasi-parent. Cole had known exactly what to say and how to say it when Peter was hurt. He had the skills.

A pinch on her hand brought Annie back to the present. "Ow. What?"

"Stop thinking about him and let's go walking in the snow after the sun comes up. Then if we can get either of our cars dug out, let's hit Pearl Street. Christmas is only a week away."

"Okay, but snowblowing, walk, then shopping."

"Shopping, walk, then snowblowing?" Jenny counter-offered.

Annie shook her head and laughed when her friend sighed dramatically.

They watched as the snow continued to fall, and the lights turned on one by one over at the Evans household, and Annie couldn't vanquish the image from her dream of Cole snuggled in a large warm bed with her beside him.

It would never happen, but it was a wonderful dream.

While the rest of his family slept in on this snowy Sunday morning, Cole crept downstairs, put on a pot of coffee and stared at his kitchen, wondering which wall could be moved to make the space bigger, more family friendly.

He pictured Annie's large modern, yet comfortable kitchen and knew his wouldn't be used for entertaining as much as hers, but a large counter like the one she'd designed could give the boys room to do homework while he puttered around making dinner.

Dinner? You rarely make dinner.

But I want to.

Mitch makes dinner.

But I want to. It's family time. It's finally time to take back my responsibility.

He realized that puttering in the kitchen also meant he had to come home earlier. Possible without a doubt, but he couldn't quite shake the sense that home also meant all the things he felt so inadequate doing, even before Lauren got sick.

When had that happened? When had he become so removed from parenting and normal home tasks?

It was too early in the day to start the kind of self-examination he knew he'd have to face sooner than later. Instead, Cole pulled a pad and pencil out of the junk drawer and started sketching, removing the wall between the kitchen and the dining room and adding a mud room to the door facing the backyard.

As he drew in a curved island with a prep sink, wine cooler, book shelves for all the cookbooks he now owned but never used, and enough seating for all four of them at the counter, Cole felt the tingle of excitement flow through him, and damn if that didn't feel good.

A large finger obliterated the new sink area he was drawing, and he pushed it aside, only then realizing it was Mitch's.

"A bit absorbed there. Whose kitchen are you designing?"

"Hey, pour one for me too," Cole said as Mitch pulled down a mug from the cupboard. "I'm designing mine. Annie amazed me with what she did to hers, particularly the big island, and I thought it would be ideal for the boys to study at while I'm making dinner."

Mitch's laugh grated only because it mimicked Cole's prior thoughts. "Hmmm, you think the boys will go hungry if I attempt to cook for them?" he asked.

"Pretty much."

Mitch poured the coffee, handing one cup to him, then

turned his chair around and straddled it, using the back to support his hands.

Cole sipped his hot brew while mentally preparing himself for the challenge he knew Mitch would put out there.

He felt almost as if he were waiting for a high-noon shootout. Instead of fingers itching to pull the gun, they were staring at each other over the rims of their cups, taking a sip, then sizing up each other again.

"Annie's kitchen?"

That wasn't quite what he'd expected, but close. The antagonism those two felt for each other had been immediate, as it had been for Annie and him. And while she had apparently changed her mind about him, Mitch's and her iciness toward each other hadn't thawed at all.

"All Josh can talk about is Annie this and Annie did that. I know she was a help when Peter got beat up, but Cole, think. She's a single woman, you're a widower with two boys. She writes children's books. It fits nicely, but so what?"

Cole frowned. "What the hell are you trying to say?"

"That Annabelle Hamilton is already moving into your life. And Josh's. Just how far are you going to let her in?"

The fire that for the last two years simmered in Cole's gut flamed up. "As far as I want her in."

"As far as being their mother? Taking Lauren's place?"

Cole hadn't thought that far, but Mitch's comment pushed his button. He'd made peace with Lauren's death at the hospital while waiting for Peter's arm to be splinted. For the first time in the two years he'd been a single father, he woke up looking forward to the day, not dreading the holiday, or feeling the intense loneliness. He looked forward to seeing Annie again, wondering how she'd surprise him.

He didn't want Mitch trying to make him feel guilty or question his actions.

"Taking Lauren's place," Cole repeated slowly. "No. No one could ever replace Lauren, but that doesn't mean I can't find a new love and the boys couldn't love another woman as their mother."

The silence between them was thick with anger. He knew Mitch still missed Lauren with an intensity that hadn't diminished at all.

Cole and Mitch had become best friends in high school, after they'd butted heads their freshman year over a science project. Usually wherever Mitch was, Lauren, younger by two years would tag along. Geek meetings, chess club and cheering them on at ice hockey practice.

Soon people dubbed them the Three Musketeers.

Somewhere along the line, Cole realized Lauren wasn't just a tagalong, she was a full-fledged woman, complete with curves, and lips that pouted or smiled to which he reacted accordingly. They spent hours talking of dreams and hopes. And they fell in love.

It was time for them to be a twosome, not an easy task with a possessive brother named Mitch. Not until the job offer of a lifetime came and Mitch moved west to Colorado.

It was the first time in their marriage that he and Lauren felt like a couple.

Mitch flew back and forth, far too often for Cole's comfort, especially after Lauren's diagnosis. But he'd never told her how happy he was when it was time for Mitch to jump back on that airplane and head to his own home.

Cole was jerked back to the present with the loud screech of Mitch's chair as he pushed it away from the table.

"Are you trying to push me out of the boy's lives? I can tell you it's not going to happen." Mitch said, standing at the table, fists clenched.

Cole stood as well and moved a step toward his brother-in-law.

"Dad? Uncle Mitch?" Peter's horrified voice stopped Cole mid step, realizing that it must look to Peter as if he were going to fight Mitch, and that he must have overheard at least part of their conversation.

He stepped back, and to his utter dismay, Peter ran to Mitch and put his good arm around him, looking up at him, a worried expression on his oldest son's face.

"You're not leaving us?" Peter asked, his voice trembling with anxiety.

Not surprising, since it was only three days ago that Peter was in the hospital, and Cole knew he hadn't quite rebounded from the fear of being in a place he didn't trust as quickly as Cole thought he might.

Josh trailed behind his brother, always waiting for Peter to lead, and Cole desperately hoped that he hadn't heard the heated exchange between himself and his Uncle Mitch.

But when he slowly walked into the room, and gravely

looked at Peter standing with Mitch, and then him, Cole knew that hope was futile and fully expected Josh to also take Mitch's side.

Instead Josh stood by him.

God, now he'd created a chasm just before Christmas that had to be healed. And the only way he could see to do this was by forcing him to make choices he didn't want to make, choosing between people he didn't want to hurt.

ANNIE FOUGHT HER DISAPPOINTMENT AS SHE HELPED JENNY brush off her car shortly after they'd finished their first cup of coffee while haggling about their plans for the day. All of it, the shopping, a walk and snowblowing was off the agenda. Jen was headed to her lab to review a new case. On a Sunday, no less.

She didn't begrudge Jen's leaving. Annie understood what it meant to have to solve a problem, take a case. That's what her dad had done, and if Annie could, she'd be there with him on the house call.

Even at that young age, Annie knew she was a storyteller and could keep kids older than herself engrossed so that the sutures weren't so painful, or the fear of the unknown when someone else was sick could take a backseat for the duration of the tale.

Nevertheless, Annie admitted to herself she'd been looking forward to having her thoughts preoccupied by someone other than Cole. Unfortunately, today it wouldn't be Jen.

The snow continued to fall gently as the storm lost its intensity. After procrastinating long enough with her third cup of coffee, Annie pulled on her snow gear and started up the snowblower.

She cleared the walk in front of Cole's house as slowly as she dared, with the hope he'd come out and talk or better yet, invite her in. Hot cocoa with whipped cream sounded heavenly.

The front door didn't open, and the vehicles in the driveway were still piled with pristine snow. Everyone was still home, and worse, the lights were on. The Evans household was up.

Stop stalling, he's not coming. Maybe the kiss did rattle him, so don't make it any worse for either of you. Get a move on.

Her inner voice was right, and anyway, how embarrassing would it be to be to be caught, as she was clearly dawdling.

Like in high school long ago when she hung around Jimmy Oppenheimer's locker, hoping against hope he'd notice her and ask her out, or heck, even acknowledge that she existed.

Well, Cole knew she existed, but perhaps a couple of good nights' sleep made him realize that a dalliance with her wasn't in his best interests. And she knew it wouldn't be more than just that.

Twice now, she'd found men who were nearly a perfect match. They'd been compatible on so many of the levels she'd thought were important. Love of children, tolerance, charity, giving back to mother earth. Laughing at themselves and with each other. A shared grin, a knowing wink.

And to one of them she'd become engaged. Ralph Holt. Beautiful man, generous to a fault, and he knew her issues.

Until his family pressured him into believing the whole blood lineage crap and he began to find fault with her determination about adopting.

Finally she handed him back his ring and could swear there was nothing but relief on his face. Hidden quickly, but there nonetheless.

And now? She didn't believe that the third time was the charm, and she didn't have the fortitude to fall in love and then face the rejection and disillusionment of a breakup because of her sterility.

A ruptured ovarian cyst in the midst of a back-country hike and the complications because of the delayed treatment resulted in a full hysterectomy.

At first she was devastated, and deeply depressed. But after a long time and with help and love from her dad and Jenny, Annie realized there were other ways to become a mother.

She'd set her heart on adopting and couldn't imagine *not* having a family until she realized that what she wanted was the whole package, not just a child.

Until Josh spent the night at her house and started her rethinking that scenario, remembering her daddy had been a single parent and she'd had unlimited love from him.

Annie blinked and realized she was still on the sidewalk in front of Cole's house.

He couldn't be the whole package; he had sons who were still grieving for their mother, but that didn't mean they couldn't be more than friends. If she could bury her heart and let them be just that.

Taking a deep breath of frosty air, satisfied with her decision, she pushed the snowblower up past Cole's house, down the other side of the street and back up to her house.

Muscles aching after putting the blower away, Annie figured a hot shower was in the picture, followed by a glass of wine, left over hors d'oeuvres, and then to her computer. An hour later, hair towel-dried, dressed back in her comfy sweats, she sat on the couch eating her early dinner and watching a few glittering flakes fall.

There was no cider duty this weekend. Come Christmas Eve, she'd be outside with the cider, but after the first weekend "unveiling," she pretty much stayed inside.

Once in a great while, someone would ring her bell and want to ask questions. Last year, she actually had someone complain about her electrical use. She'd been able to jolly them up by telling them she had solar panels on the shed in the backyard and sold that power back to their utility company.

As if she conjured the sound by her thoughts, the doorbell rang. It wasn't even five o'clock, but the storm made it feel like the dead of night.

"Hello," she welcomed as she pulled open the door and summoned a smile.

Then stared dumbfounded at the man who hadn't left her thoughts all day.

"C-Cole," Annie stammered.

He raised a brow. "Yep, it's me."

Gathering her scattered wits, Annie gestured him in, but he stayed outside.

"I can't stay, we're on our way to Macky auditorium for the Holiday Festival and have an extra ticket. Want to come?"

Then she realized his Pilot was pulled into the driveway, motor running. She could make out Josh and Peter in the back seat, and no one else. Which meant no Mitch.

Was this wise?

Friends with benefits?

Heck, it was Christmas and Christmas music was her favorite.

She looked down at herself. "Do I have five minutes?"

"Two."

"Yikes, then see you in two."

She closed the door, ran up the stairs, threw on a black cashmere sweater and jeans, swiped on another lick of mascara, threw on her black boots and grabbed her purse.

She was in the car in two minutes flat.

Cole smiled appreciatively.

"Annie, it's great you can come," Josh said from the back seat.

Turning in her seat, she surveyed the boys. Josh wore a wide smile and Peter barely smiled at all.

"I'm glad I was invited. Peter, how's the arm?"

"Okay."

All right then. "When do you get your proper cast?"

"Dunno."

Just before she turned back, she noticed that Josh punched Peter in the thigh. Boys.

SITTING IN THE PILOT, WAITING FOR THE POST-CONCERT traffic to clear, Cole hummed under his breath. The concert had been magical. Macky's stage had been lit with all sorts of lights and decorated with Christmas trees. The music and last sing-a-long brought home the spirit as little else did ... except for Annie's lights.

Was it really only two weeks ago that he'd thought her light display was going to be a nuisance? An eyesore? A detraction?

Now the lights were comforting to see when he came home, and to take one last look at before he went to bed.

Yeah and see if her room lights are on are, wondering where she is in the house, or if she's snuggled up in bed.

The traffic began to move, and Cole wasn't ready to return home yet. The night was too magical to end. "Anybody up for dessert at the Cheesecake Factory?" he asked.

"Me!" Josh said.

"Peter?" Cole had been trying hard not to let his son's sullen behavior since breakfast ruin the outing.

"Sure."

"Annie?"

Cole looked at her, willing her to accept, wanting her to

be with him. And being with him, more often than not, would include the boys. It might as well start now.

"I can't. I promised myself that I would get the first half of the illustrations for the book done by tonight and I have two more to go."

"Aw, Annie, can't you do them tomorrow?"

"Nope, I'm way behind schedule. I'm sorry kiddo, how about a rain check?"

Cole stopped for a red light and glanced at her, wondering if she was trying for that "taking it slow" concept she'd mentioned. She met his gaze, and he saw genuine regret for having to refuse the invitation.

"Can we watch you draw sometime?" Josh asked.

"Sure."

"Tonight?"

"How about this coming week? You're off from school and I'll be home a lot."

Cole pulled into her driveway and watched as Annie got out and waved goodbye. He waited until she was inside and then headed back down the hill to the Pearl Street Mall and cheesecake.

"I'm glad she didn't come," Peter said.

"Take that back," Josh yelled.

Cole pulled over to the curb, then turned to look at his older son. This wasn't the time he'd have chosen to have this chat, but Peter had gone too far.

"Annie is a friend and a neighbor. I like her, Josh likes her. The fact that you don't puzzles me. She's done nothing to alienate you."

"Uncle Mitch thinks she's after you. That she could be our new mother."

Peter's face scrunched up in anger, but Cole saw hurt confusion in his son's eyes.

"First off, Uncle Mitch doesn't know what he's talking about, and second, I'm not looking to find you boys a new mother."

"But you like her. You've never been like this before."

"Yes, Peter, I like her. Liking and marrying are a far way apart on the scale of a couple's interaction."

He wanted to assure his son, knowing Peter wanted him to say, *don't worry, it's not going to happen*, but he couldn't.

Annie had gotten under his skin, and Cole just couldn't lie to his son.

8

MONDAY MORNING AND DAY ONE OF THE BOYS BEING HOME for two weeks, and although it meant that Cole would have to take off work, he hoped Mitch got his phone message last night asking him not to come over today. They needed to cool off from yesterday's confrontation.

Additionally, Cole had to figure out how to handle Peter's disturbing and nearly outright declaration of disliking Annie.

As he headed downstairs, Cole smelled the deep roasted scent of coffee brewing and was pretty darn sure the boys hadn't made it, so he knew his wishes weren't to be granted.

Sure enough, Mitch paced the kitchen, mug in hand.

"Didn't get my message last night?"

"I did. How was the concert last night?" Mitch asked.

"Really wonderful. The boys and Annie enjoyed it as much as I did, though Annie sings better than any of us."

Cole poured a cup and headed to his office to make a call, telling his crew he'd be in late, maybe not all day.

Since Mitch was here, and the boys were still asleep and couldn't overhear as they did yesterday, Cole might as well have the talk now with his brother-in-law about Peter's mistaken assumption that his dad was going to remarry anytime soon.

"Annie was there?"

Cole sat behind his desk, barely suppressing his sigh.

"I invited her since you weren't coming."

Mitch placed his cup down carefully on the desk's mahogany surface and narrowed his eyes.

"Sit down, Mitch, you're aiming for a talk and I agree we need one."

"I don't need to sit down. I got here early because I want to make sure you understand that I wasn't kidding when I told you that I'm not giving up my rights to the kids. Your phone message—"

"Rights?" Cole couldn't believe what he was hearing. Mitch had no rights to the kids.

"Poor choice of words, Cole. You know what I mean."

Yes, I know exactly what you mean.

"Mitch, I'm not planning on falling in love, but if it ever happens, nothing takes away the fact that you're their uncle, and they love you."

The man paced the small floor space of Cole's office as he had in the kitchen, fraying the tenuous hold Cole had on his temper.

"Sit down," he said, using the same sharp tone he used with the boys when they were acting up.

Apparently it worked because Mitch finally sat.

"We need to talk about the boys, especially Peter's bent to engage in fighting."

Mitch's stare could have bored holes into Cole's brain.

"And what is wrong with standing up for what is right?"

Cole opened his mouth, but Mitch interrupted him.

Here it comes.

"Lauren could have had a fighting chance if you'd stood up to her. Pushed her higher on the donor list by moving to another state if necessary." He jumped up and resumed his pacing.

He stopped in front of Cole's desk, placing both palms flat on the wood, leaning over, practically in Cole's face. "She could have had a fighting chance."

Mitch whirled away, but not before Cole saw the shimmer of tears.

"The boys have to learn to stand up for the people they love. That's what Peter was doing. You want them to be wimps—"

"Like me, is that what you were going to add?"

Mitch turned and Cole saw the agony and anger in his eyes, his jaw set, his hands balled into fists. "If the shoe fits."

He wants me to come at him so he can finally work out the anger.

"I'm not going to fight you, now, tomorrow, or ever. And don't forget, Lauren's treatment wasn't handled by anyone but her and her doctors." He held a hand up as Mitch was about to interrupt.

"Moving, in her opinion, wasn't an option. Just as not being able to accept your kidney right away wasn't an option. Nobody knew that she'd have cascading organ failure during her treatments, waiting for her rejection antibodies to be cleared."

"At least I offered to donate."

Cole sighed deeply, he wasn't going to air the conversation he'd had with her about him donating. "Mitch, I loved Lauren with all my heart, I wanted to crawl right into that casket with her, but I had the boys to think about—"

"You haven't been much of a father either."

Let's air it all out, then.

"I agree, keeping the family cohesive was Lauren's domain, though we talked over issues, but it was Lauren who mostly handled it."

"Because you didn't want to."

"No, that's not it at all." Cole didn't want to have this conversation, now or ever, but guessed it had been festering inside Mitch by all his taunts in the past couple of years. "Lauren was with the boys more than I was, you know that. Research was taking me all over the world. The boys needed to understand that Mom was boss, but that we agreed on the method of taking care of them. They didn't often play the *Mom said ask Dad* card."

Cole raked his hand through his hair, wishing he hadn't missed so many workouts these past few weeks. The endorphins kept him sane at times like these.

"Mitch, I know you're still grieving—"

"What? And you're over it already?"

Now definitely wasn't the time to tell him about the peace he'd made with Lauren's death.

Mitch looked at him suspiciously. "It's that woman next door, isn't it?"

"Don't be childish, you sound like Peter. And her name, as you well know, is Annie."

Mitch glared at him, then stormed out of his office.

Just bloody fantastic.

The front door slammed.

Hearing lighter footsteps running down the hall, followed by the door slamming again, Cole brushed off the worry over Mitch and followed the steps of Peter. He had no doubt it was him, and sure enough, Peter was struggling with his splinted arm, but succeeding getting into Mitch's SUV.

Thank God, Mitch was smart enough not to drive away with Peter in the vehicle.

Trying to keep his temper under control, Cole pulled open the door.

"Peter, Uncle Mitch is leaving, and I think you should head into the house."

"No."

Cole glanced once at Mitch and saw him swiftly cover his triumphant expression.

This ended now.

Not the best time, being the holidays, but Cole would take time off and find a way to handle the boys without Mitch.

"This is not open to discussion. In. The. House. Now."

Peter glared at him and sullenly stormed into the house, slamming the door behind him.

Only then did Cole speak again.

"This isn't working. I'm not keeping you from seeing the boys, you're doing a fine job yourself." He closed the Jeep's door and followed Peter into the house, closing the door, wondering just how many doors he was closing at this moment.

It wasn't Annie's fault, but Cole didn't see how he could spend time with her with this crisis going on.

9

"GIVE IT BACK. ANNIE GAVE IT TO ME, IT'S MINE," JOSH cried.

"It's stupid," Peter yelled. "It's a baby toy."

"It's not stupid. Give it back."

The boy's yelling rang through the house and Cole had enough.

He stormed into Josh's bedroom to see Peter standing on the bed, holding the plush star high above his head, taunting Josh.

"Enough. Both of you." Cole moved toward the bed, ready to take the plush toy from Peter.

"If Josh wants it, he can fight me for it."

Shock stilled Cole's feet. "What?"

"Finders keepers."

Josh jumped trying to reach his toy. "You took it. It's not finders if you took it."

"Stop." Cole said, fury punctuating that one word. He

didn't care. The boys' arguing had escalated for the last three days and this tension was becoming a nightmare.

Squabbling was expected but this was intolerable.

"Give me the toy. Now."

"I miss Uncle Mitch. Why isn't he here? Did you send him away for good?"

"No, he's free to come if he wants to. But who would want to come over to this noise?"

Peter gave him a disdainful look as he held the toy toward him, then dropped it just as Cole put his hands on it.

Cole handed the star to Josh, who stuck his tongue out at Peter.

"I've had enough. I don't know why the fighting has gotten so bad, but enough. Stay in your rooms until dinner."

"Uncle Mitch wouldn't make us do that," Peter challenged.

"Uncle Mitch isn't your father and I am."

"I wish he was," Peter said under his breath.

Cole chose to ignore it, but the barb struck.

"Dad, it wasn't my fault," Josh whined.

"Both of you."

Cole stood in the hallway, arms crossed, waiting as Peter took his time getting to his room. He felt more like a policeman than a father.

Maybe Mitch was right, maybe he wasn't cut out to be a father.

Peter slammed his door, Josh slammed his, and Cole went to the kitchen. It was only Wednesday.

LOWERING HIMSELF ONTO THE OAK CHAIR, COLE TIPPED IT back on its two rear legs, and stared up at the kitchen's popcorn ceiling, hating everything about it.

He wanted to take a sledge hammer to it right now and work out his frustrations. Get a good sweat up and get those endorphins pumping, helping him think clearly on what to do about Mitch, the boys and Annie.

The fight he'd just stopped between the boys and Peter's taunt about fighting Josh forced him to give them time apart. But that wasn't really a solution, it was just that, a time-out for all of them.

The annoying front doorbell pealed its antique series of cheesy chimes, then stopped.

Then pealed again.

The doorbell would have to go as well.

Cole didn't feel like moving and certainly not answering the door. Maybe what he needed to do was seek out some help about the boys. Surely there were single parent groups he could attend?

What you really need is a good ear. And that would be Annie. Someone who understands kids. Hell, admit it, what you want is her smile, her whiskey eyes lighting up with joy. That woman radiated joy.

One more peal of the bell.

What the heck, maybe chatting with a neighbor or even a solicitor would take his mind off his failings.

Opening the door, the object of his needs stood there in a traditional ivory woolen ski sweater, skin-tight black leggings and boots. No jacket, no gloves, and it had to be all of three degrees outside.

"Annie."

"Cole," she said with a grin, then shivered.

He realized she carried a basket, with cellophane-wrapped somethings tied with ribbon nestled in the towel lining the wicker.

"I brought the boys some of my cookies and fudge. And for you, my infamous rum balls."

Cole grabbed her arm and pulled her inside.

At her stunned look, a chuckle escaped him. Damn, it felt good after this last hour of drama.

Glancing at the staircase leading up to the second floor landing and not seeing any heads poking through the railings, Cole felt less guilty, then furious that he should feel any guilt at all over having Annie in the house.

Nevertheless, it was better if they moved into the kitchen so they could have a bit more privacy in case the boys decided to break their time-outs and investigate who had been at the door.

He took Annie's basket and led the way into the kitchen. "You're a sight for sore eyes. I've got coffee on, so we can sample those rum balls."

SERIOUSLY? COLE THOUGHT SHE WAS A SIGHT FOR SORE eyes? Then why had he been nearly invisible since Sunday?

Annie had noticed that Mitch's Jeep hadn't been

parked around the house, so maybe Cole was taking sole care of the boys. That would explain his fervent comment. He needed a life preserver and she was it.

Grinning as she followed him into the kitchen, she found little had changed since Cole moved in except the room felt more lived in.

The aluminum rimmed, yellow linoleum table where she'd sat often with her ancient neighbor, reliving times past, was gone, replaced by a round butcher block table and five chairs.

Books were stacked haphazardly on the counter, multiple sizes of boots were piled in the corner near the back door, and the single maple book shelf next to the refrigerator was now loaded with cookbooks, not knick knacks as it had been with old man Thompson. The room felt alive, even vibrant with the chaos on every surface.

"Sorry the coffee is simply drip, but it's hot and it's Sumatran. Does that make up for the fact it's only basic old coffee?" Cole asked as he poured a cup.

"You bet. Do you have any cream?"

"Half and half?"

She nodded and watched as he added a dollop, stirred and handed her the mug. She smiled as she turned the mug around to survey the hand-decorated "I Love Dad" painted on the surface.

"Who did this one, Peter or Josh?" She held up the mug to Cole.

"Josh."

Cole's heavy sigh indicated things weren't smooth at the moment in the Evans household. She'd guessed right so far. "Try a rum ball, and then if you want, tell me all about it."

"You come bearing gifts of food and you're a mind reader. I couldn't ask for more."

Yes you could, Annie thought as her blood thickened and her pulse quickened. *A lot more.*

Cole picked a powdered-sugar covered, rum-and-cocoa treat from her basket, put the entire nugget into his mouth, and instantly his eyes glazed over with pleasure.

He picked up another and it went down as quickly.

Annie had always heard that the way to a man's heart was through his stomach, and apparently it was true. "I gather you like these," she said, reaching toward the powdered sugar clinging to the corner of his mouth.

Kissing it off, as she wanted to do, with desire running through her veins, wasn't a wise move, at least at this moment.

Her movements slowed as his blue eyes suddenly brightened and glittered as if he knew exactly what she was thinking. Two mind readers in the room was scary ... and exciting.

The kitchen blurred while Cole stood before her in sharp masculine focus. The sleeves of his polo shirt were pushed up to his elbows, showing firm, muscled skin, giving her fantasies about the other taut muscles of his body.

Letting instinct move her, Annie gently wiped one corner of his mouth with her index finger, delighted when his lips closed around it.

She moved closer, nestling her leg between Cole's as he sucked the last bit of sugar off her finger.

She pulled it slowly from his lips, cheeks burning as erotic images of other acts played in her mind.

His blue eyes deepened as he cupped her face and leaned toward her.

"The boys?" she murmured.

"Banished to their rooms," he whispered against her lips.

"Why?" Annie heard her voice, low, sultry.

"Squabbling about everything. Peter took the toy star you gave Josh and was teasing him with not giving it back."

"Hmmm, sounds like average kid stuff."

"Enough talking," he whispered as he finally claimed her mouth.

She'd been waiting for a replay of the kiss they'd shared days ago. This one was better, they both knew it was coming, it wasn't a surprise. But in no way was this kiss less heady than their first.

Blood thrummed in her ears, and her knees trembled.

Cole inched forward, pressing her back against the counter. She was trapped in the most delightful way possible.

His strong but gentle fingers stroked up, then down her back, the wool of her sweater scratchy on her sensitized skin. She wanted to pull it off and the camisole underneath, and have his fingers on her bare flesh.

As a starter.

Again, being the mind reader, he reached under her sweater, beneath her silky camisole and caressed up and down her spine. Cole touching her so intimately while she was still dressed felt like snatching forbidden fruit. Exciting, delicious and tempting fate.

It was tit for tat time.

Wrapping her arms around him, she tugged his shirt from his jeans and returned the torture, with hands playing up and down the planes of his bare back.

Getting no resistance, she wiggled her finger under the waistband of jeans, feeling the small of his back, but couldn't go farther. His belt stopped her exploring fingers.

She sighed into his mouth. He raised his head just enough so he could form words. "Pity, isn't it."

"In many ways. I guess I shouldn't pull off my sweater and rip off your shirt," she taunted.

"No. Which is indeed a pity."

Pressing against him, she felt his arousal. He was as much turned on as she was. *Indeed, a pity skin couldn't be next to skin.*

Cole's lips brushed hers again, and she closed her eyes, narrowing her world down to just that, his lips on hers. Firm and cool as he tasted her, teasing open her lips, as if he wanted to take her wholly in the only way he could at this moment.

Then he released her mouth, keeping her tight in his embrace.

She turned her head, resting her cheek on his chest, feeling its rise and fall as he steadied his breath.

Still pressed against the counter, she had nowhere to move and didn't want to.

This kiss wasn't the ordinary prelude to the next step,

this kiss went deeper, it involved emotions she didn't want intruding on the relationship. It felt a lot like falling in love.

At least it did for her.

Damn.

Cole tilted up her head so she had no choice but to meet his gaze. "You felt it too, didn't you?"

Well, she could lie, but was pretty awful at it. "I did, and it scares me."

10

"I scare you?" Cole asked. He was certain Annie had felt all he'd felt during that kiss, and being scared was not part of it.

Stepping back a few paces, he stared at Annie, willing her to explain.

"Cole, I didn't mean scared, I meant *scared.*"

"Well, that explains it," he said, earning a chuckle from her.

He was relived when Annie closed the gap he'd created between them and stood toe to toe.

"Yeah, I know, good with words, and I'm the writer. It's just that relationships never seem to work out for me, and it's usually my fault."

Nothing could have astounded Cole more.

"How on earth could it be your fault? You're the most giving, honest, friendly, and sexy woman I've met in years."

He was rewarded as her arms snaked around him and

she laid her cheek against his chest again. It was right that she be there, touching him.

He rested his chin on top of her head and closed his eyes, savoring the closeness of the woman next to him.

Not any woman would have given him the same sense of home, of completeness, and that thought astonished him.

Making his peace with Lauren's death had given him the closure he needed, letting him know just how much his life had been on hold.

Feeling this sense of unity with Annie was unexpected.

The rational scientist in him said he should step back and analyze the feeling, check the data, see if it made sense.

The human male side argued that this was good, even wonderful, and why bother to fight something that seemed right.

"Do you want to tell me what you really mean by scared?" Cole asked softly.

Annie looked up at him, her eyes troubled as if she were waging a war inside herself.

"Maybe, maybe soon, but not right now. Actually, what I'd like to do is share another kiss."

"That's certainly easily granted."

Fighting off the slight disappointment that she couldn't confide in him, Cole lifted her chin and covered her lips again, feeling the same rightness and undeniable electricity between them.

He cupped her buttocks and pulled her closer to him,

his own desire swelling, growing hard. He knew she couldn't help but feel his need. Was it too much? She'd been the one to say take it slow. Is this what scared her?

Annie didn't pull away as he drew her closer.

Cole was suddenly overcome with the need to possess this woman in his arms. It wasn't that he'd been without sex for over two years, it was that he wanted to protect her, wanted to take away whatever was scaring her. To make her his.

It was a primal instinct he'd never felt before, coursing through him, and he held her tighter as if he could shield her with his body, his soul.

Annie broke the kiss. "Wow, I thought maybe the first kiss a couple of days ago was a fluke. No fluke."

"And?"

"Hey, Dad. I'm hungry," Peter's voice came from the living room.

Annie darted backward and busied herself playing with the basket she'd brought.

Cole moved to the sink, fighting to calm himself and his body.

"Dad, I'm sorry about Josh," Peter said as he walked into the kitchen. "Cookies? For us?"

"HEY, PETER. YUP, FOR YOU GUYS," ANNIE SAID, unwrapping the cookies she'd brought. "I needed to get away from the book for a while, so I hit the kitchen. I made fudge, chocolate chip cookies without nuts, because Josh told me you both liked them that way, and for your dad I made some rum balls."

Annie watched Peter glance from her to the cookies. The boy was warring between acknowledging that she brought something he'd enjoy eating and the fact that she was somehow the enemy.

Finally he looked at his dad for permission. Cole nodded once, obviously still unhappy with what happened.

Peter took a cookie and stuffed half of it in his nine-year old mouth.

Annie waited anxiously for the verdict.

His eyes lit up and he stuffed the rest in. Cole pulled a glass from the cupboard, milk from the fridge and filled the glass, handing it to him.

"Thanks, Dad."

"Can I have another?" Peter asked Annie.

"Fine with me, if your dad says it is."

Cole nodded. "Sure, then go tell Josh he can come down as well."

Peter took another big bite, a gulp of the milk, and ran out.

"Well, you may have a new friend," Cole said.

"I'm not surprised that he's been a bit standoffish."

"He's been rude. I'm sorry."

"I think it has to do with his mother." Annie braced herself for the conversation that would surely follow. They hadn't talked about Lauren yet, and now she'd brought up the subject.

"You're right."

He cupped her cheek, but the intimate gesture did nothing to relieve Annie's tension.

"Lauren loved kids. A houseful was part of the plan. For a while it was Josh instead of Peter who took her death the harder ..."

Cole's words faded away. *A houseful was part of the plan.*

Those seven words smashed her little dream world, and she had no one to blame but herself. She'd known this was coming, courted it, so to speak. Even Jen had said this would be nothing but trouble. Cole was a widower who'd lost the love of his life and the chance to have that houseful of kids, along with two boys who still missed their mother.

Buck up, girl. Enjoy this time, make it work for you and Cole and the boys, be that friend with benefits, for all of them.

Annie tucked her heart back into its hiding place.

"... now it seems to be Peter who's struggling with Lauren's death. He overheard Mitch saying that maybe I was thinking of replacing her with you."

"Yeah, well, that would do it," Annie interrupted, pushing her heart deeper into its cave. "Poor Peter. No one can replace his mother. And even if you remarry, Lauren is still his mother. Nothing can take that away. He needs to know that."

"I thought he did, but apparently Mitch has been feeding some pretty heavy guilt trips on the kids."

"Ah, and Mitch doesn't like me."

"He has no right not to like you."

That was an awesome remark for Cole to make. Annie

wished she could move back into the warmth and security of his arms, but the boys would be uncomfortable with that.

She heard excited voices and forced a smile.

Just before they burst into the kitchen, Cole tucked a folded paper square into her hand. She tucked it into the basket without looking, but curiosity was killing her.

"Annie, you made our favorite." Josh burst into the kitchen and made a beeline to the basket.

"They're good. Better than Uncle Mitch's," Peter said.

Over the boys' heads, Annie met Cole's amused glance. Uh-oh, one of those shared moments.

"Dad, what are we having for dinner?"

"Cookies? That's your fourth."

Peter grinned, and it transformed the boy.

"No, really."

"I don't know. I haven't given it much thought."

"Pizza," Josh suggested.

"No more pizza for at least a week."

"Let's go to McDonalds," Peter said.

"Taco Bell," Josh chimed in.

"How about Wahoo's, and eat healthy?" Cole said. "Want to join us?"

Annie smiled at Cole's beseeching face, but shook her head. Peter's slight thawing toward her felt like an important breakthrough and she didn't want to push the "off" button on it.

"Guys, I'd love to go out, but if I don't get my illustrations done, and I've been distracted," she risked a glance at Cole and got a quick grin in return, "I'm going to be in trouble."

She got a pout from Josh, a look of surprise from Peter, and a frown from Cole. Putting the rest of the cookies on the festive tree-shaped plate she'd brought and setting the red tin of fudge next to it, then handing the small tub of rum balls to Cole, Annie was done. She hooked the empty picnic basket on her arm and moved toward the door. "Enjoy dinner."

Cole joined her at the front door and leaned against it, blocking her way. "That's twice you've refused my invitation to dinner."

"Both times, the book, promise, it's not you. I'd never kiss a man I wouldn't have dinner with." She leaned toward him. "Truthfully, it's Peter this time, he definitely softened toward me, and I don't want to blow that," she whispered.

She braved his skeptical look.

"Will you have dinner with us sometime?"

Remember, enjoy these moments. "Like I said—"

He glanced behind him, then bent and captured her lips.

Damn him. It was delicious, a mix of rum, cocoa, coffee and Cole. Annie wanted to cling to him and let the kiss sweep her away.

Double damn him.

"Just something for you to dream on tonight. I know I will," he whispered into her ear, then opened the door.

Triple damn him, she didn't want to leave, ever.

And staying wouldn't be an option once Cole was enlightened about the true Annie.

LEANING BACK IN HER OFFICE CHAIR AND STRETCHING mightily, Annie looked at the last illustration on her artist's drawing table, swiveling the board's center section, checking her work at all angles. It was perfect. Glancing up, five new illustrations were on the magnetic storyboard above her table. Damn, but she'd done a lot of work this evening.

But then you had a fantastic incentive.

"Yes, I did and now I can take a peek."

Annie had used every ounce of discipline she had and made herself wait until she got enough work done that she could take a break. The note from Cole was resting on her kitchen counter, next to her coffee machine. If she'd left the folded square of paper in her office, she'd have been tempted to take a peek. But now the note beckoned, along with a cup of coffee and maybe a rum ball or two.

Fixing a tray, she carried all to the living room, clicked on the remote for the gas fire and watched as the crushed glass below the dancing flames reflected the light.

Enough waiting, torturing herself wondering what the note said. It could simply be a thank you or a phone number. It was time to find out.

Unfolding the paper carefully, scrawled in handwriting that was just legible, was a phone number which she'd guess was his cell. Below that an email address and then finally what she was hoping for, *Dream of me. I'll be dreaming of you. Sleep well, sweet Annie, C.*

It was short and sweet, but wonderful. She hadn't had a love note since high school.

Love note?

Well, maybe not, but it was pretty darn nice.

It could be a love note.

You don't want a love note.

Liar.

"No, I'm not. Facing rejection isn't worth it," she muttered putting an end to her internal argument. "Still, it was nice."

Annie pulled out the laptop she always kept stashed in the living room in case she got an idea and wanted to write it down before she forgot, and brought up her email program.

Almost giddy with fear and excitement, Annie copied in his address and typed.

Dearest Cole,

Then backspaced through that. Too much.

You've filled my dreams every night since we met. Sleep well, Cole. ~ A. She added her cell number.

Her finger hovered over the send button for a second, then she closed her eyes and pressed.

If Cole wanted to answer, he'd now have her email address to do so.

A few minutes passed and no answer. She drank the coffee, ate the rum balls and stared into the fire.

Maybe she'd said too much in her email.

Unable to stand the suspense of whether he'd answer

or not and feeling foolish that she cared so much, Annie pulled on her parka and headed outside, hoping her Christmas lights would work their magic and soothe her agitation.

Nearly all the other houses on the block were now lit with twinkling lights and the neighborhood glittered white, red, green, yellow and blue.

It was magical and she felt the joy of the season creep in to replace the anxiety.

Finally the night's subzero temperature sent her back indoors, but not before she took one more glance at Cole's house and now saw a light shining in the room she'd assumed was Cole's.

Hoping she was right, Annie dashed up the sidewalk and through the door.

The new mail icon was blinking. *Email comes through my cell. Did you get a lot of work done?* she read.

Nearly all complete. One or two more and it's ready. Oh, and the cover. Sorry I woke you. She typed quickly, heart beating fast.

It's the best way to be woken up. Are you going to be up much longer?

Nope, though I just had a cup of coffee. I've got shopping to do, three days before Christmas.

Where are you going? I need to get a few things for the boys as well.

Pearl Street. Starting early, coffee first, then binge shopping. I'll call you. Sweet dreams.

You too. G'nite. Annie waited another minute, but nothing more came over email. She signed off her computer and yawned. Still smiling over the note and the texts, she climbed the steps to her bedroom and glanced out the window to a dark house next door. Then she tumbled into bed, sweats and all. Knowing she'd dream sweet dreams of Cole.

11

THE RUCKUS AND RUMBLING FROM THE BOYS' ROOMS WOKE Cole.

He dreaded another day of squabbling, and had been racking his brain to find something outdoors for them to do, a fun activity that would wear them out. Skiing was out of the picture with Peter's arm and although Mitch had promised them a day of learning how to ski at Eldora over Christmas break, it wasn't going to happen for a few months.

Throwing on sweats, Cole headed for his home office, knowing he'd have about ten minutes to Google activities for a boy with a broken arm that would be safe.

Surprised to find the light on in the living room, Cole cautiously walked in.

Mitch sat in one of the wing chairs, wearing snow gear.

"I thought you'd figure Peter couldn't ski with his arm."

"I did and 'figured' I'd take them snowmobiling instead. I thought you wouldn't mind."

"Ah, that's what the early morning noise is all about. They're getting ready."

"They're going to be pretty disappointed if you say no."

"Then maybe you could have checked with me first." Cole didn't want to rehash any of the last two meetings with Mitch until after Christmas. There were going to be changes, but rocking the boat this close to the holiday wasn't something he wanted the kids to deal with anymore than they had.

"I should have, but the deal came together at the last moment. Karl has two snowmobiles. He'll take one of the boys and I'll take the other. We'll be back by four."

Mitch's admission took the wind out of his sails. He wasn't a bad man; in fact Cole still thought of him as his best friend. Lauren's death changed them all, and it was time to get back on solid ground with him.

"Start-up wizard Karl?"

"One and the same."

Cole couldn't help his look of disbelief. Karl was vegan, wore clogs and held his long blond hair back with a rubber band.

Mitch laughed, and it felt good to hear his laugh again.

"I know. I was surprised as well. We're heading to his dad's ranch in Breckenridge."

"Dad, did you hear? Snowmobiling!" Peter yelled, running down the stairs, dressed in his snow gear.

Cole smiled. "Did you help Josh get ready?"

"Yup, he's right behind me."

"Gloves, hats, mufflers?"

Peter and Josh showed him their gear.

"And we're going to McDonalds for breakfast. We're eating in the car."

Cole shook his head at Mitch. "You're crazy."

"Yeah, but it's a drive to get there, and it's faster this way."

"Bye, guys, have fun."

"Bye, Dad, see you later."

He waved at the boys as Mitch's Jeep headed up the street and turned onto Baseline and swiftly moved out of sight.

Cole glanced at Annie's house. Her Lexus was gone. She wasn't kidding when she'd said she was getting an early start.

After a quick shower, he stood staring at his closet. Dressing with more care than usual, he chose gray slacks, a black sweater, a white shirt, and then put down the tie he'd automatically plucked from the rack. Maybe the East Coast was beginning to wear off.

Feeling just a bit nervous, as if this was a first date, he called Annie's cell, hoping she'd answer and would want to meet to go shopping.

In less than fifteen minutes—and only because it was so early—he found a spot to park and was walking down the Pearl Street Mall to Broadway, The Unseen Bean and Annie.

As he pulled open the coffee shop door, the aroma of freshly ground beans filled the air, and he breathed deeply. He spied Annie sitting at a table for two in the middle of the café, smiling and waving him over.

She'd been watching for him. That alone filled him

with a sense of belonging to someone, and made him feel as if they were a couple.

He didn't shy away from the warmth that notion imbued him with.

"What, no peppermint latte?" he asked, sliding into the chair across from her.

"Their coffee all by itself is heaven—wait until you try it."

Cole went to the counter and returned a few moments later with his own steaming cup.

"What's on the agenda?" Cole asked, admiring Annie's red sweater. She wore a silver star pin, and her hair was mussed in a way that looked like she'd just woken up.

He groaned at the image of her in bed beneath him ... and moved on to another part of her face, or else he'd be in big trouble.

Her whiskey eyes twinkled with merriment. Vibrant and filled with joy as she was, why would she be interested in an old stuffed shirt like me? Cole wondered, staring at her until she coughed.

"What?"

"Your coffee is getting cold. Stop staring at me and start drinking."

Obeying orders, he sipped, then sipped again. "Wow, you're right. Good."

"Speaking of good, you look pretty darn good yourself. No tie?"

"God, woman, stop reading my mind. I almost put one on but stopped in the nick."

He reached across the table and laced his fingers in hers. It felt right.

In fact, other than at the hospital and the school, this was the first time they'd been together in public.

She drew circles on his hand with her index finger. They sipped from their cups simultaneously and then shared a grin. "Spooky," Cole said.

"Wrong holiday. But I know what you mean. I like it."

"Me too. Back to my original question, what's on the agenda?"

"I have to pick up a pair of earrings that Jen has been lusting after forever. Some gifts for the neighbors. And a couple of frames."

"Frames?"

"Well, I guess those depend on your answer."

She had him totally intrigued. "About?"

"If it's okay with you, I thought I'd draw Peter's and Josh's favorite character de jour as a little Christmas gift. You should know which ones they like most, and I'll practice so when they come over, I can draw it while they watch."

He didn't know their favorite character, damn it all, but he would in the future, he swore.

"You're a generous soul, you know that, right?"

"Cole, I'm not buying them BMWs, just a little drawing for Christmas. I want to be sure Peter doesn't think I'm trying to bribe him."

"He ate two more cookies before bed. You have a fan."

"I can make more. Where did you want to shop?"

"There's a kite store near here. Know it?"

They left the coffee shop and headed toward the mall. Cole hadn't spent much time there, in fact practically none, other than getting the set of body bars for his home gym.

The sun reflected off glistening snow piles. The middle four blocks of downtown had been turned into a pedestrian mall, and additional shops and restaurants stretched for blocks on either side.

Garlands and banners adorned the black lamp posts. The trees, branches bare of leaves, would be magical at night when lit, but not as magical as his very own light show next door.

"There's an ice skating rink down 13th Street, if you want to risk skating," Annie said, pointing.

"Risk? I played ice hockey with Mitch in high school, and then I played through college."

"Is that so? I learned to skate on the pond behind our house in Maine. I bet I'm better."

He loved the challenge in her voice. "Is the rink open now?"

"I think so."

"Then you're on." Cole grabbed her hand and headed down the street. The newly cleaned ice beckoned and the skate rental hut was open.

In no time Cole had his hockey skates laced up, Annie had her figure skates on, and they were gliding across the hard surface, cold air nipping their noses.

He hadn't skated in a couple of years, but the instinct was still there, and at the moment the ice was all theirs.

It felt good, skimming across the frozen surface. Annie

skated in circles around him, managing to cut right in front, yet miss colliding.

"Eat your words, Cole," she yelled, then got up some speed and did a jump, twirling in the air, then landing perfectly.

He applauded as did the bystanders who'd stopped to watch.

Skating backwards, Annie bowed to him and the crowd.

Cheeks pink from the frosty air, Cole realized that Annie wasn't simply pretty, she was stunning, self-assured and talented. He couldn't believe she wasn't married with a passel of kids.

He blinked, returning his attention to the moment. "Too bad we don't have a net here, or I'd show you some fancy foot work. I was the 'deke and dangle' king in college."

"So, you were great at faking, eh?"

Cole pretended to be wounded. "Faking? Try deception, detour, but fake? Never."

Annie grinned, and skated around him, then did another pirouette and some fancy move where she skated on one foot, her arms outstretched, head up like a bird gliding across a frozen pond.

He leaned against the metal railings and watched her. Taking a deep, chilling breath of the clean air, he felt reborn, revitalized.

She skated over to him, breathing rapidly. "Wow, I'm out of shape. You're not breathing hard at all."

"I work out."

"How could I forget?" she said, a twinkle in her eye.

Damn if he didn't want to bend and capture her lips right now, press her against him, feel her heartbeat thrum, but the rink was beginning to fill with kids off from school for the holiday. Cole settled for linking arms as they slowly glided around the perimeter to the rink's opening. They sat down and slipped off their skates. At the rental counter, the return of their own shoes brought them back to the real world.

"That was fun, thank you," Annie said, relinking her arm through his. "We should bring the boys down."

Cole stopped dead in his tracks. That sounded so good.

Annie's gloved hand flew to her mouth. "I'm sorry, that sounded presumptuous and I didn't mean it that way."

"Why not? It's a great idea."

"I'm not involved with them on that level."

"You could be," Cole said.

ANNIE STOPPED AT COLE'S SUGGESTION, HER BOOTS GLUED to the icy pavement. A group costumed in old England garb mouthed lyrics to Christmas carols she didn't hear. The crowd passed her and Cole in a blur of color.

Wouldn't a family be the best Christmas gift of all?

And isn't that pretty much impossible?

Her heart yearned for the image Cole painted. A myriad of pictures danced through her head: the frenzy of a Christmas morning with the boys, skating at the rink together, the aroma of their favorite cookies baking. Being a part of the boys' lives—fixing boo-boos and stopping fights.

Fights. Mitch.

His name splashed icy reality and doused her dream. But she couldn't bring herself to squash it completely, nor could she bring herself to wipe that hopeful longing off Cole's face. Echoing the longing in her soul.

Quickly composing herself, Annie retreated into her usual jovial demeanor. "Wow, that is some great offer."

"I'm serious."

"I know you are, but it's early in this whole thing, don't you think?"

"Maybe, but I don't think you really mean that. Nevertheless, I'll wait."

Seriously? He really did mean what he'd suggested. Her heart fluttered and she pulled down her sunglasses, using the pretext of shading her eyes from the sun's glare sun on the snow so he wouldn't see the deep yearning his offer created.

Linking her arm through Cole's, she pulled him down the mall to the next block and to the Italian designer clothing store that had the earrings Jen so coveted.

While the willowy and impeccably dressed clerk wrapped the small box, Annie tried on the cashmere shawl she'd lusted after the last time she'd been in the store. She watched Cole from beneath her lashes, but he seemed to have no interest in the gorgeous clerk, paying close attention to her instead.

Jen's gift was ready. Annie reverently placed the shawl

back on the stand and slipped the gift bag securely onto her arm, then led Cole to the kite store he'd mentioned.

Cole listened to the young clerk's enthusiastic dissertation on the merits of one kite over the other and picked four kites, then another.

Annie stopped by the Boulder Arts and Crafts Co-op and finished her shopping.

Laden with bags, they were done. The mall was crowded now, not surprising since only three days remained till Christmas Day.

Annie heard Cole's stomach growl and after the third restaurant they'd passed that had a waiting list of thirty minutes or more, she decided to take the risk. "I can make us hot turkey sandwiches with gravy, and I have more rum balls, if you'd like to have lunch at my house."

He groaned. "Sounds fantastic. You're on. I'll meet you there."

Annie turned to head back to her car, only to be stopped as Cole turned her around, bent and brushed her lips with his.

"See you shortly."

COLE WIPED HIS DAMP PALMS ON HIS JACKET, TOOK A BREATH, then another, and finally, courage in hand, rang Annie's doorbell.

"It's open," she called.

Hanging his overcoat on the craftsman-style coat rack in the foyer, he headed toward the kitchen. Pausing after he got there in order to admire this woman who, in the matter of a few weeks, had become incredibly important to him.

Annie efficiently pulled out a cutting board, selected the right knife from the magnetic rack over the sink and quickly ran it over and under the knife steel.

"It took you a while. I was worried you'd gotten lost," she said with a smile.

"I had a bit more to do. And then traffic." He raised his hands palms up. "Did I miss lunch?"

"What kind of hostess would I be if I didn't wait for my guest?"

She'd put on a bright green apron with ruffles, all the more strange because Annie didn't seem to be the ruffle type of woman. She'd slipped off her boots and wore fluffy black slippers. Her trim and utterly sexy ankles peeked from beneath her skin-tight pants, showing every curve and dip.

He sucked in a quick breath, not realizing until that second he'd been holding it.

She whirled around, knife in hand and he read; *One Wise Woman Beats Three Wise Men Any Day* embroidered on the front of the apron. Clever.

"Um, do you think you could put the knife down, just for a moment?"

She did and he let instinct carry him on, wrapping his arms around her, nuzzling her neck.

"Woody, citrusy and," he nuzzled again to find that other scent, "musk."

"You're very good. It's Chanel°5."

"Good choice on you." Cole raised her chin and took her mouth in a long, hard kiss.

Her hands tunneled through his hair, gripping tighter, bringing his mouth impossibly closer. He slid one leg between hers; it was as close as he could get while dressed.

"You said the boys were out, so I'm guessing no interruptions, at least for a couple of hours," she murmured against his mouth.

"Indeed."

"Indeed. Have you seen what your house looks like from my bedroom?"

"Not yet. Am I about to?"

Her lips parted and he watched her breasts heave as she breathed quickly. "If you're sure about this."

"Yes, aren't you?"

"Absolutely."

Annie took his hand, and they climbed the stairs to her bedroom. Kneeling on the window seat, she raised the blind. "Which room is yours?"

"Directly across."

"I guessed that."

"Because?"

"I've seen the lights go off, then the curtain moved. I don't think Josh or Peter would be looking out the window in the dead of night unless they were looking for Santa."

"Guilty."

"Not yet, but I'm thinking we're aiming at changing that."

Sudden doubt filled Cole. He'd not been with a woman

other than Lauren in more than a decade, and he wanted this to be perfect with Annie.

As if sensing his unease, the beautiful woman kneeling beside him wrapped her arms around him, pressed her cheek to his chest.

"Your heart is beating pretty fast for a man as fit as you," she said.

"Different stimulus."

"Ah, that explains it. Lift up your arms."

He did as requested, and Annie pulled off his sweater and began unbuttoning his shirt. His doubts fled as she stroked each inch of bare skin she uncovered, then kissed where her hands had touched. Cool fingers followed by burning lip—it was an exquisite sensation.

"Not fair."

She raised a brow.

"You're fully dressed."

"Which you can remedy."

He untied her apron and pulled it over her head. She still kneeled on the window seat; Cole stood. "Your turn, arms up."

He kept his gazed locked with hers for the instant it took to pull off her sweater and reveal her wisp of red lace. He looked down and swallowed hard. "That should be illegal."

"Possession is nine-tenths of the law."

So he did. Cupping her breasts with both hands, he held their weight, felt her nipples bead, heard her breath catch.

Scooping her up, he slowly carried her the few feet to

the bed and gently lowered her to the white duvet. "Now we're even."

Annie smiled and held out her arms. Cole lay beside her.

Running a finger over her breast, and watching her bite her lip, the desire to possess her filled him as it never had before.

His mouth replaced his finger, his tongue laving her nipple through the scrap of lace covering it.

She arched beneath him, then writhed as his fingers trailed downward, past her stomach, to the apex of her thighs, stroking, teasing.

God, he was so turned on, and they were still half dressed.

Needing to slow down a bit, Cole trailed his fingers back up to her belly button and looked for a zipper to release her pants, but couldn't find one. There was no way to pull off those skin tight trousers.

"Side. Zipper's on the side," Annie said between gasps.

He found it and yanked it down, as fevered as Annie, slowing down be damned. "Lift your hips a bit."

She did, and he pulled down her trousers, revealing another scrap of red lace. With her hips nearly in his face, the sight was almost enough to break him.

He rolled away for a moment, unzipping his trousers, kicking them off. He'd put on black briefs this morning, liking them much more than his standard issue tighty-whiteys.

Looking back at Annie, he saw appreciation glimmer

in her eyes, beneath her slightly closed lids, giving her a sexy, come-hither look.

Damn straight he was well on his way. Shifting so he was on his side, he propped up on one elbow and devoured her body with his gaze.

"Enough, my turn."

Annie pushed him down and mimicked his prior pose as she swept his body with her gaze. He got harder.

She smiled.

"Wanton woman."

"Indeed."

Cole slipped off her panties, the scrap of red lace barely covering his hand, then reached around and unhooked her bra, pulling it off her shoulders. It landed with the other scrap on the window seat.

"Again you have the advantage," she whispered.

She reached to remove his briefs, but he knew if she touched him, he'd be lost. Quickly staying her hands, he kicked off that last barrier between them and settled over her body.

"Your choice, slow and tender or fast and hard."

"Fast and hard now, slow and tender later."

Thank God. Cole didn't think he could handle more foreplay and keep it together.

Annie shifted under him, and just as he was ready to join them, reality hit.

"Damn, I didn't bring protection."

"Don't worry, I'm safe."

"You're certain."

"Positive."

Then as if to make sure he understood, she grasped him and guided him to her. One thrust and they were joined.

Exactly as it should be. Making love with the woman Cole was growing to love.

12

Annie snuggled deeper against Cole's warm chest and into his arms. She listened to his strong heart beat and his even breathing and realized he was sound asleep, in her bed.

How wonderful.

She pretended this could be real life, that she would wake up to Cole every morning, curled up like this.

Opening her eyes for a minute, it took again as long to realize it was now dark outside. The sun had set.

Glancing at the clock, she shook Cole, then jumped out of bed, gathering his clothes, trying to see if they were wrinkled, thus tale-telling.

God, his white shirt was a mess, but the black sweater should hide most the evidence.

"Annie, what are you doing?"

"It's after four."

He stretched, and she admired his bare chest, ripped

abs and strong arms. Who knew a scientist could be such a specimen of beefcake?

She'd felt almost every inch of his body. They'd made love twice, falling asleep entwined and waking the same way to begin the magic dance again.

"Wait, did you say it was after four?"

She smirked. "Yep, Einstein. Get moving. When are the boys expected home?"

"Any minute. Can I use your shower?"

She pointed to the adjoining room. While Cole showered, she pulled on leggings and her favorite sweatshirt from Disneyland. Mickey and Minnie celebrating Christmas, shyly about to kiss under a sprig of mistletoe.

Annie grabbed a fresh towel from the linen closet and handed it to him as he exited the steaming glass-enclosed alcove.

"Do you want to leave your packages here? Or are they safe in the car?" she asked.

Cole pulled on pants, shirt and sweater. "Safe from prying eyes for the time being, but thanks."

"Hair. Wet. Dryer on second shelf."

"What? Oh yeah. Thanks."

He plugged in the dyer and ran it until his hair was nearly dry. It didn't escape her that this all felt very domestic. And while she'd had her fiancé, Ralph, stay over a few times, it had always felt as if he was intruding on her space. Mostly they spent time at his place.

But this felt right.

Cole fit in, too darn perfectly.

Annie blinked and watched Cole put on his boots.

"I'm sorry the day has to end like this, in a hurry—furtively almost," he said.

"It's fine."

Cole paused and as she looked down, avoiding his eyes, she felt his gaze searching her face.

"No it's not, but it can't be helped," Cole said.

"Exactly."

He gathered her into a hug, resting his chin on the top of her head.

God it felt so good to be wrapped in his warmth—for a minute she felt she belonged there, as if they were a couple.

"Don't dismiss this as an afternoon delight, Ms. Annabelle Hamilton. It was much more than that for me."

Damn him. She couldn't be what he wanted.

The breath she took faltered as she tried to draw it deep into her lungs.

She followed him downstairs, each step heavier and slower than the last.

Cole turned at the door. "I'm not kidding, this was ... heck, it was amazing, and I want to feel this all again, every night."

He gathered her close, kissed her deep, drawing her heart out of its protective shell. Leaving her vulnerable.

Then he left.

I want to feel this all again, every night, he'd said.

What that did that mean in real life?

Something she wouldn't dwell on, for Annie was sure, once he was back in his fold, he'd think twice about the magnetism that drew them impossibly close for a few hours. Then he'd dismiss it as being caught up in the season's magic.

And you?

Oh, I'm caught up all right. Now how do I make that magic lose its hold?

THE MINUTE COLE WALKED IN THE DOOR, HE COULDN'T avoid Mitch's accusing stare.

"Your hair is still damp," his brother-in-law said, tone flat.

Damn if Cole was going to feel like a teenager caught sneaking in late after a tryst. This wasn't a tryst and he wasn't a teen.

"Drop it, Mitch. It's none of your business. Where are the boys?"

"Taking their baths."

The accusing tone was too much. "I'm glad you got them started."

"And I ordered Chinese. It should be here in about ten minutes."

Cole forced himself to walk out of the kitchen calmly and not let Mitch know just how much he was annoying him. That only seemed to make it worse.

He'd hoped things were going to be a bit smoother after this morning's reasonableness.

Climbing the stairs, he heard the excited voices of his sons and realized how much he'd missed this day-to-day routine. Lauren had seen to their baths and tucked them in, reading them bedtime stories, until Peter got too old for it.

Oh yeah, Cole had kissed them goodnight, but it was Lauren who insisted on getting up when they cried with a nightmare or were ill.

Standing stock still on the second floor landing outside the Jack n' Jill bathroom, Cole realized that Lauren's insistence that she be the mother to the children went beyond normal parenting. That she needed to be indispensable to the kids because she hadn't experienced that kind of selfless love herself.

She'd had Mitch and Mitch had her, while their parents spent every cent they could lay their hands on either gambling or for another get-rich-quick scheme.

Lauren had made it her mission to be there for the boys. Cole had heard the term helicopter parent, and maybe she'd been exactly that.

Cole realized he'd done nothing to interfere with her routine. It seemed to work for all of them.

But now a sourness crept into his throat that he'd been missing this part of the boy's lives.

And if he let Mitch take over Lauren's role, he'd never have the closeness he realized he desperately wanted.

The bathroom door opened, letting out a billow of steam. Emerging from the cloud, Josh, already dressed in PJ's, nearly bumped into Cole.

"Dad! We had an awesome time snowbiling."

"Snowbiling? Good word. I want to hear all about it over dinner. Uncle Mitch ordered Chinese."

"I know, I got extra egg rolls."

"Hey, Dad, guess what?" Peter asked, bolting from his room.

"What?"

"Uncle Mitch thinks he can get you a snowmobile cheap."

Keep your cool, Evans. It's not Peter's fault, it's Mitch's.

"Really? Wow, we'll have to talk about that one."

Peter's face fell.

"Talk about it, Peter. I didn't say no."

"You will."

Probably.

"Maybe not. If it was fun, then it's worth thinking about seriously."

The doorbell rang, and he heard Mitch talking to the delivery person.

"Dinner's here. I want to hear all about your adventures today." Cole ignored Peter's surprised look.

Things were going to change around here, starting now.

OVER DINNER, COLE TAUGHT THE BOYS HOW TO USE chopsticks, and though they abandoned them in favor of forks pretty quickly, Cole kept using his. The boys watched him in between talking about the "snowbiling" and hinting for Christmas presents.

Peter picked up his chopsticks and tried again, laughing when all the rice fell off, again surprising Cole. It seemed he hadn't heard Peter's squeal of laughter in months.

He worked hard to keep the boys' attention off the fact that Mitch was sullen, worried that the man would make some nasty comment.

They opened their fortune cookies, and Peter held up the white slip from his. "Ask and you will receive," he quoted. "Hey, Dad can we talk about the snowmobile now?"

The rumble in Cole's chest exploded into full-fledged laughter. "Good timing, son." Cole turned to Mitch. "Tell me about this snowmobile."

Mitch pulled a creased flier out of his pocket. "Saw an ad in the paper yesterday and the guy sent me this in an email."

Scanning the flier, Cole got to the bottom line pretty fast. "Eleven grand for a used snowmobile? Seems steep to me."

"See, I told you, Dad won't even think about it."

Mitch smirked.

Cole's fuse shortened. They'd committed to spending Christmas Eve and day at Mitch's house, and Cole wouldn't back out of that, but once Christmas was over, things were changing fast.

"Peter, I didn't say no—it's just pretty expensive. I know you can't ski right now, but I thought you were pretty keen on that new pair of skis and boots. You'll be back on the slopes this season."

"That's a long time off, Dad."

Cole nodded, folded the paper and laid it beside his

plate. "I understand. I'll think about it. Maybe we can rent some snowmobiles or use Karl's again and see?"

He expected a surly nod from his son, but got a half-smile instead.

He'd take it.

The boys finished with their meals and asked to be excused. Cole gathered up the empty cartons and tossed them, then put the plates in the sink.

Mitch just sat there.

"Spill it."

"Just wondering if you're going over there again later tonight. Sneaking off while the boys are asleep."

Cole's fuse blew. "Don't be an ass. I'd never leave the boys alone. You need to stop this now. My relationship with Annie has nothing to do with you."

"It has everything to do with me. Lauren, your wife, my sister, is gone. I'm not going to let the boys forget her as you apparently have. They were her world."

Forgotten her? Cole gritted his teeth, struggling to stay calm.

Mitch picked up Josh's abandoned chopsticks, then put them down as if they burned his fingers. "I don't get you. You, me and Lauren were always tight. Even after you two got married we hung out together. Then the boys came and I got the job here. But we were still close. And then Lauren got sick—"

"And you didn't like the way I was handling it," Cole interrupted. "Lauren was an adult, don't forget. She made her own decisions about her care. She didn't want to die and was ready for the transplant when her body was.

Nobody thought she would go as quickly as she did. Nobody was ready for it, not I, you, nor the boys. But life moves on. Making the boys think badly of any other woman I either happen to like or look at twice is unhealthy, as is trying to bribe them with gifts or tell them that fighting for what's right is the only way to stand up for what you believe in. I won't have that."

Mitch scraped his chair back so fast, it fell over. Cole watched as the man curled his fists. Black tension filled the kitchen.

"I suppose you're going to back out on Christmas Eve as a lesson to me?"

"You suppose wrong. But after the holidays there will have to be some changes."

"Like I said, you're not keeping the boys from me. They're my only tie to my sister."

The agony in Mitch's voice tore through Cole. "That's not my intention, but as I said Monday, you're doing a good job of it without my help."

Once again, Mitch left the house without another word.

Cole reached for his cell, typing a message to Annie. Only after he hit send, did he realize she was his first thought for comfort, for advice.

It was still early. He hoped she was still awake.

Got a minute to talk? Cole's text read.

Annie had all night. After he'd left, she made a hot

turkey sandwich for herself, and poured a glass of pinot grigio. Then, only picking at the sandwich and ignoring the wine, she'd restlessly wandered the house, not liking the sense that she didn't feel complete unless Cole was with her.

Making love with him had been something completely different than she'd ever experienced with another man, not that she'd had a huge number of men to compare Cole with.

Even fast and hard had been tender, filled with lightning touches that seared her even as he moved to the next aching spot.

Her friends-with-benefits concept was fully realized with Cole, yet it felt like a sham. She wanted more than that from him.

But more wouldn't happen, and she reminded herself that she must drop the idea right out of her heart.

They couldn't make love again unless he knew all about her friends-with-benefits idea and agreed.

He'd probably be totally on-board with her concept. Jeez, what man wouldn't?

What's up? Annie texted back.

Issues with Mitch and the boys. Just seems overwhelming, so I thought of you. Today was pretty special.

Annie read Cole's reply three times, her heartbeat accelerating with each pass.

I thought so, too. Did that have anything to do with the "issue"?

A bit.

Tomorrow I have a signing at the Boulder Bookstore, but

Saturday afternoon I'm free. Want to send Josh and Peter over early Christmas Eve, and I'll draw them their Christmas presents?

Great idea. Peter mentioned your cookies. We're out.

Annie chuckled and mentally noted to bake some more Saturday morning. *Okay then, how about three?*

We don't have to be at Mitch's until later, so that would be great. I found out it's Iron Man for Josh and Optimus Prime for Peter.

A pang went through her at the thought that she'd be alone again this Christmas. Jenny's new assignment took her to Washington, DC, and she said she might not make it back in time, so please hold Christmas until she got there.

You can't hold Christmas. It's its own magical day. But they would exchange presents later and Annie would make their traditional fettuccine Alfredo.

Okay. I'll brush up on the characters. Anything else I can help you with? She quickly texted back so she wouldn't lose this link with him.

A good night kiss?

Again, her heart accelerated and warmth pooled in her stomach.

I think this will have to do. XOXOXOXO. G'nite, Cole.

'Nite, sweet Annie, no worries that I'll dream about you.

13

TIME TICKED AWAY AND ANNIE WAS RUNNING BEHIND FOR her signing. She'd overslept after staying awake long past midnight reliving the nearly three weeks since meeting Cole Evans, PhD.

Rushing through her shower and getting dressed, she blessed her lucky stars that she always planned what she was going to wear the night before. Today it was black stretch pants tucked into low boots, a green sweater with snowflakes and snowflake earrings.

Smiling as she swiped on mascara and liner, she carefully applied her trademark red lipstick. She only wore it at signings or photographs, because it made her feel invincible.

Running two yellow lights, she pulled into the alley behind the Boulder Bookstore only to find her reserved parking spot had been taken by, she supposed, a frantic Christmas shopper who couldn't read "reserved for signing author" on the sign.

She squeezed the Lexus next to the "Employee of the Month" space, thankful that the employee drove a small Prius. Annie ran up the alley, around the corner to Pearl Street and the bookstore.

Taking the stairs two at a time, breathing hard, she surged past a line of people. She reached her floor and was stunned to find the line snaking up the stairs and around the landing led to her signing table.

A few children stood with their parents, but mostly it was adults who wanted her to sign their child's gift.

An hour and a half later, her hand was cramping, the books on the table were nearly gone, and a cup of coffee sounded like manna from heaven.

Signings were magical. Every year her sales got better and now with the plush toys license, she couldn't imagine where in the world her *Star Light, Star Bright* books would be read and who might go to sleep with one of her stars tucked in beside them. It was heady and it kept the smile on her face as she looked up to the next person in line.

"I heard a telepathic SOS for a peppermint latte."

A flush started on her cheeks, burning all the way down to her toes.

"You are a magician." She took the cup, sipped and sighed. "Where are the boys? Get it worked out with Mitch?"

"Nope, I left them downstairs in the kids' books section, so I can't stay but a minute."

"A minute is awesome," she whispered for his ears only as the line began to form again behind him.

Cole stepped aside and she had a moment of déjà vu

about the night she'd first lit the lights and asked him to step aside.

She signed two books for each customer, a grandmother from Nebraska and a young girl who was getting them for her sister. Annie also signed a postcard for the girl, who apparently was so excited to meet her that she clutched the card to her chest and forgot the books for a moment, then ran back to retrieve them.

"Fans of all ages," Cole commented.

"Maybe I should start writing 'tween books."

Cole glanced behind him, then bent over the table and bussed her cheek with a kiss. "I've got to go, but we'll see you tomorrow. I'm going to be selfish, but dream of me, sweet Annie."

And he was gone before she could respond. It was only early afternoon, but she'd bet any amount of money that tonight's dreams would once again be filled with Cole.

She sipped her latte and signed the last of her books, far outstaying her two-hour signing slot.

Looking up, she saw Mitch standing against a book stack, frowning at her.

She blinked and he was gone.

Had it been her imagination? Was Mitch following Cole and the boys?

COLE STRETCHED OUT IN THE ONLY COMFORTABLE CHAIR that would fit in his small home office. Heck, why not just call it the den. Home office sounded stuffy, even East Coast.

He grinned at the thought. The last three weeks had changed him in countless ways. And today had turned out pretty darn well, just him and the boys.

Peter and Josh had behaved, for the most part, and he'd bought them each an early Christmas present of a book from the bookstore and one for himself as well.

Seeing Annie in her element made him so proud this woman was a part of his life.

He ached with the need to be with her, joined in the most intimate way.

He never thought it would be possible to fall in love again, in fact had avoided even the notion of it.

One, because he hadn't yet made peace with Lauren's death, and two, he didn't want to go through that kind of pain again. Losing someone, watching them suffer while he could do nothing.

But that night in the ER while waiting for Peter's arm to be splinted, he also realized that trying to protect himself from hurt was naive and impossible.

He wasn't omnipotent and hadn't been able to keep Peter from being hurt, and consequently, himself.

Cole rose and detoured toward the bar in the living room. After pouring himself a Knob Creek on ice, he headed to his room. Then backtracked to grab the book he'd bought today. On the way to his bedroom, he realized he'd left on every light in the house. Annie had pushed aside the darkness he'd felt better living in.

He'd turn them off just before he went to sleep.

Sleep? He was too keyed up to sleep. Plans needed to be gone over once more to see if every angle was covered.

For tomorrow was Christmas Eve.

The boys were excited about Christmas, excited to eat cookies at Annie's and see the surprise she had in store for them.

Tomorrow was also the day he was going to suggest that he and Annie *not* take it slow.

Cole ran through the scene.

He'd get the boys from Annie's around five, hand Annie her present, and whisper his suggestion in her ear. Then wish her a Merry Christmas, steal a kiss and skedaddle out of there.

A text should arrive on his phone within minutes.

Christmas Day, after they got home from Mitch's, they'd have a light dinner and together tuck the boys into bed.

Then wine in front of the fire—no, make that champagne in front of the fire. To celebrate the season and their new relationship.

What could go wrong? Nothing. He'd looked at all angles of the equation. He was sure Annie felt the same way about him.

Feeling more lighthearted than any time since moving to Boulder, Cole peeked out his bedroom window to see the lights on in Annie's, but the blind was drawn. No matter, he had the image of her sitting on the window seat etched into his brain.

Switching on the bedside lamp, he settled down with his new book to finish the evening.

His fingers itched to text her, but if watching her work today's crowd at the bookstore exhausted him, he'd bet she would soon be snuggled sound asleep under the sheets they'd so recently shared.

Groaning, he opened the book to take his mind and his body off the woman next door.

14

THE LAST BATCH OF PETER'S FAVORITE COOKIES HAD FIVE minutes left in the oven.

The house smelled of rich dark chocolate, smoky coffee, raw sugar—Annie's secret ingredient in her cookies —and Madagascar vanilla.

She'd already set up her hot cider stand in the carport for this evening's crowd, and all the ingredients were in the pot on the stove, waiting for her to turn on the burner and let the heat meld the flavors.

Cinnamon, cloves, oranges and apple cider. It was her daddy's recipe, as was his tradition to have a pot simmering on the stove in their Maine woods house. If he was called out for an emergency, Annie had learned at about Peter's age to carefully fill the thermos with the cider as Daddy got his bag and they headed out together.

Together they worked, Annie telling stories to keep the family from fearing the worst as her daddy healed their loved one.

She missed him the most at Christmas and understood that Peter and Josh must be feeling the same about their mother.

Annie sat at her kitchen counter, waiting for the timer to ding, sipping from her mega coffee cup, watching as the flakes began to fall.

Snow always felt like a new beginning, blanketing everything in a coat of virgin white.

No tracks to mar it yet, no dirt or soot. Just white, with splashes of green from the firs and pines layered up the mountains above her house.

Christmas Eve and snow. What could be more perfect?

A husband to share this moment with. Kids crazy with the anticipation of Santa's arrival.

The oven timer dinged and the doorbell chimed.

Quickly pulling the cookie sheet out and placing it on the cooling rack, she ran to the door, hoping Cole was bringing over the boys.

Flinging open the door revealed only the boys. Annie tamped down her flash of disappointment. "Merry Christmas Eve. Come on in."

"I could smell the cookies before you even opened the door," Peter said, a gleam in his eye.

"Me too," Josh chimed in. "Can we have one?"

"You can have a whole plate full with either milk or hot chocolate. Which will it be?"

"Hot chocolate with whipped cream?" Josh asked, hope ringing in his voice.

"You bet. And Peter?"

"May I have milk?"

Annie hung their coats on the coat rack, gathered all the goodies onto a tray and carried it up to her studio as the boys followed. Festive Christmas music played softly from her computer speakers. She already had a couple of bean bag chairs in the room and put the tray on a low table in front of them.

"Did your dad tell you what I planned?"

"He kinda did," Josh said. "He's not good at secret-keeping. You're going to draw for us. Show us how you make your ill ... us ... tradions."

"Close, illustrations." Annie smiled at the image of Cole trying to be tight lipped, then blurting it out.

"But it's a bit more than that. I'm going to draw a picture just for each you. Who wants to go first?"

"You mean of whatever we want?" Peter asked.

"Yup, like your favorite super hero."

Peter's eyes gleamed with excitement.

"Let Peter be first," Josh said.

Annie fell harder for the young boy. How sweet.

"I get my cast on Monday, Annie. I get to pick my color."

Was it only a week ago that Peter wouldn't even say two words to her, and now was volunteering information?

"Let me guess." She screwed up her face, pretending to think hard. "Red and blue for Optimus Prime?"

Peter just stared at her. "How'd you know?"

"Annie knows almost everything," Josh said.

Annie laughed hard. "Oh, I wish that were true, but you just keep on believing it."

"Can you really draw Optimus Prime?"

"Sure, it'll be my version of OP but I think you'll like it. Do you want him transformed as the truck or as the Autobot?"

"Can I have both?"

"Sure, we should have time, right?"

Peter nodded. "We don't have to be home until after five."

He stood at her shoulder while she drew Optimus Prime as the tall leader of the Autobots.

"Wait, you left off the flames on his fenders at his feet," Peter said.

"So I did, and I think I left off a couple of other things too."

She rapidly drew the flames, but she couldn't remember the details of the armaments on his shoulders.

"Can I have a piece of paper and maybe I can help you remember."

Handing him pencil and paper, she sat him on the floor to draw.

He scrunched his face in deep concentration.

"Can you draw my favorite character?" Josh asked.

"Sure. What is it?" Annie pulled out a fresh sheet of watercolor paper and waited with her pencil poised to draw Iron Man.

"Maximus."

"My Maximus?"

"Yup." He looked at her shyly. "Is it okay?"

Josh must have seen the puzzlement on her face.

"Of course, Josh. I just figured you for an Iron Man type of guy. Can I ask why Maximus?"

"I like Iron Man a lot. He saves people, just like Maximus does with Jeffrey and the puppy."

Josh looked at Annie, his eyes wide and serious. Glancing first at Peter, Josh moved closer to Annie, and whispered in her ear.

"I want to find a star so I can look up and find Mommy."

Annie ached for the little guy. "Josh, if you find a star, it won't be your mommy. Remember I told you that you'll just feel like she's closer because you can remember her when you look at the star. The star will always be there for you. Do you understand the difference?"

"I think so, but you said we all have stardust in us, so wouldn't Mommy be in the star?"

Annie pulled Josh closer. "No, sweetie, but that's a very smart thought. It works the other way around. We have stardust in us. The stars left it here. They don't have human particles in them, but because they left the stardust on earth billions of years ago, they have that special connection with us."

Josh thought for a moment, then nodded wisely. "Still I like Maximus, *and* Iron Man."

"Then let's draw them working together."

Josh grinned hugely and Annie started drawing.

"Hey, is anybody home?" Cole called after opening the door, left unlocked, to Annie's home.

Not really worried about the door but curious why the

boys were so late in returning home, Cole approached the steps leading to Annie's office.

Mitch followed closely on his heels.

"Hello?" Cole called again. He heard Christmas carols and Josh's high-pitched laugh.

Annie darted out of her office, a startled expression on her face.

"God, you scared the bejezzus out of me. What's up?"

Mitch stepped from behind him, and Cole saw contempt fill her gaze as she glanced at his brother-in-law. Somehow they'd moved from icy to downright hostile. What had happened?

"You left the front door unlocked, so I came in. The boys are late," Cole said, pushing aside that worry.

Peter peeked out of the office behind Annie, wearing a guilty expression. "Hey, Dad, Uncle Mitch."

"Did you tell Annie you needed to be home by five?"

"By five? I thought you said after five," Annie said, looking at Peter.

"I kinda did say that."

Cole fought the grin that wanted to break out at Peter's answer; he had such a hangdog, caught-in-the-act tone. Instead, Cole crossed his arms, trying for a stern expression, while secretly thrilled that Peter *had* fudged on the time. Maybe Mitch's hold was loosening.

Josh appeared in the hall, standing close to Annie, and again Cole's heart leapt. This was all going according to plan.

"Well, I guess that's okay, but only because I knew where you were. Did you have cookies?"

"And hot chocolate and milk. And guess what Dad? Annie drew us our Christmas presents. I got Iron Man and Maximus! And Peter got Optimus Prime, but he asked for two pictures, and the second one isn't done yet."

"Yeah, can we stay a bit longer?"

"Cole, wait, what time is it exactly?" Annie asked.

"Five-thirty."

"Oops, I've got to get the cider on."

"Annie gives cider to the people who come to look at her lights," Josh said to Peter.

"Cool, can we help you?" Peter asked.

"Maybe another time, Peter. We've got Christmas Eve at my house, remember?" Mitch said.

Peter's look of indecision delighted Cole. *Amazing what chocolate chip cookies combined with Annie will do.*

"I can finish OP tonight and give it to you tomorrow," Annie promised Peter, then shooed everyone downstairs.

Cole grabbed the boy's coats while they snagged another cookie and Annie turned on the burner beneath the cider pot, drumming her fingers on the counter.

"You know what they say," Cole said.

"Yeah, yeah, a watched pot."

Cole itched to gather her into his arms, and wish her a Merry Christmas Eve, but not in front of the boys, not yet.

And Mitch was watching him like a hawk eyeing its prey. Cole needed Annie alone.

"Mitch, why don't you and the boys head on over to your house and I'll follow in a minute."

Mitch hesitated, then must have realized Cole wasn't

going to take any crap. He grabbed their jackets and headed out the door with the boys in tow.

Cole gathered Annie into his arms and took her lips with his. She pressed her body into his, and his reaction was swift and hard.

"I'm sorry we won't be together this Christmas Eve, but, Annie, I'd like to change that in the future."

Her eyes gleamed with mischief. "You're planning next year already?"

"I'm planning my life. With you in it."

She stepped away, and Cole sensed she was putting more than physical distance between them.

"I thought the friends-with-benefits was working out nicely."

What the heck? A tendril of unease began to curl in his stomach. "I'm not sure what friends-with-benefits really is, it sounds like a convenient new term to categorize casual sex, but this is feeling like a whole lot more than sexual."

Annie turned back to her stove and watched the cider simmer, then turned off the burner.

"It can't be."

"What the hell does that mean?"

Annie wouldn't face him.

This was not going according to plan. Grasping her shoulders, he turned her to face him.

She wouldn't look at him, but he'd be damned if she'd put this kind of distance between them without seeing the truth in her eyes.

"Why are you suddenly putting up this barrier?"

"I'm sterile."

The pain in Annie's two words tore him apart.

He gathered her close. She was hurting from this revelation and he wasn't sure why. That she loved children was undeniable, but there were other ways to become a mother.

"And?" he murmured into her hair.

"I can't have children."

"And that makes you what? Less desirable, less lovable?"

"Yes."

"That's crazy. For such a sane, wonderful woman to believe ovaries make or break her, I don't get it. Who told you that?"

"It doesn't matter who said it."

"Of course it matters. Petty people—"

"My fiancé for one. Not so petty."

This must be what it felt like to be sucker punched. "Your fiancé?"

"Ex-fiancé. Practically left me at the altar after his family convinced him the Holt's gene pool had to be continued at all costs. Adoption wasn't an option."

"So one man convinced you—"

"It wasn't one man. I heard it from people whom I trusted. That I was now different."

"What bullshit. For a smart woman—"

"Hey, I thought you'd like that idea."

"What, that I would simply be a convenient sex partner? Why would you think that?"

"Because it's simple and uncomplicated. You have the boys to think of. This way our relationship doesn't impact them."

"What if I want it to impact them? You're looking at only one part of a big, multifaceted relationship."

Annie sagged against the stove.

Thinking quickly, looking at all angles, Cole decided to play his last card.

"What about being a mother to my children."

Bleakness filled Annie's eyes. Not the excitement he'd expected to see shining there.

"Cole, I can't be a mother to your children."

He wanted her to repeat that, but couldn't bear it if what he heard was correct. Annie couldn't have said anything more devastating.

Standing before him was a woman who oozed kid appeal, and he'd been sure she loved children.

And maybe she does, just not your family.

No, she'd always been wonderful with the boys. As much as he was hurting, he had to give her that.

Cole thought he heard a sob, turned, but saw nothing, except the front door standing ajar.

"Would you like to explain that? I thought you enjoyed Peter and Josh." *And me.*

"I do. This isn't about them or you, it's all about me. Selfish? Yes. Even more reason you should either run away or stay and enjoy being friends—"

Cole held up his hand. He couldn't hear that phrase one more time. It wasn't his style and he knew, deep in his heart, it really wasn't Annie's either.

"Listen, I better get outside with the pot of cider. The crowds expect it."

She grabbed her parka from the coat stand and pot holder mitts from the drawer. "Would you get the door for me?"

Annie made the moment sound all so normal, and it sure as hell wasn't normal. He held the door open for her when what he wanted most was to slam it shut and keep her inside until he got answers that made sense to him. And not the stupid friends-with-benefits line ever again.

Instead he did as she asked. "Sure."

He intercepted her uncertain look and steeled himself not to react. It was she who was creating this distance and now wasn't the time to solve the problem.

Maybe never was the time.

Closing the door behind him, he watched as the line formed the minute Annie and the cider appeared.

And as it had that Sunday three weeks ago, snow was falling.

The lights were magical, and several young kids had books clasped tightly in their mittened hands. Annie was ready with a pen to sign them. Such a gracious woman who believed the lie she'd been fed about herself. Damn those people.

"Merry Christmas, Annie."

She looked up from the book to stare at him, and her eyes filled.

"Merry Christmas, Cole."

She turned back to her line and he felt dismissed.

How could his plan have finished so badly when it started with such promise?

Pasting on a smile, Annie handed out another cup of cider. Her lights still shone brightly, illuminating the snow as it fell. But the magic of the season fell flat, even dark, as Cole walked away.

She desperately wanted to believe that Cole would be content with the family he—they'd—have now, but she couldn't risk it, especially after he and Lauren had wanted a houseful of kids.

And to make it worse, it would be more than she who got hurt, it would be the boys. Annie remembered just how hard it had been when her mother left her and Daddy.

Her cell phone vibrated in her pocket and she grabbed it, hoping against hope it was a call or at least a text from Cole.

But it was Jen, telling her how bleak Washington was and that she was eating a bowl of fettuccine Alfredo in the hotel restaurant as some jackass at the bar was trying to pick her up with the lame line that they'd met before.

Jen signed off with x's and o's and the promise to call tomorrow.

Christmas Day.

The crowd admiring the lights was dwindling, getting ready for their Christmas Eve, and Annie had nothing to look forward to but the next morning. Empty.

A few presents under the tree, which was nice, but not the same as having kids squeal with delight, a lover with which to share the morning and snuggle up with into the night.

Annie glanced at her watch, surprised it was past eight p.m. Time to wrap it up.

Carrying the nearly empty pot inside, she returned to her table to grab the last of the cups and napkins. Tomorrow she'd take down the tablecloth and fold away the table. She wasn't in the mood to do more than have a glass of wine or heck, maybe scotch, and stare at her fireplace and brood.

Locking the door behind her, she turned off the foyer lights, grabbed a tumbler of Chivas and watched the lights on her tree twinkle and the fire dance among the crushed glass.

Snow continued to fall, and usually she felt comfortable in the seclusion the veil snow offered. Tonight she felt lonely, and a headache pounded in her head.

It took her a moment to realize it wasn't only the headache pounding, someone was pounding on the front door.

She didn't want to face anyone. Annie knew she'd blown whatever slim chance she'd had with Cole and all she wanted to do was be alone.

Angry at herself, she slammed the glass down so hard onto the coffee table she was amazed the crystal didn't shatter.

What the heck was wrong with her? She hadn't been this destroyed when Ralph Holt pulled the world he'd offered from beneath her feet.

"Annie? Open the damn door."

Cole? His voice wasn't angry, or accusing, it was scared. What happened?

Jumping off the couch, she ran to the door and flung open the door. Cole strode in, followed by Mitch, who looked as if he'd like nothing more than to wring her neck.

What was going on?

"Where is he?" Mitch asked, getting right in her face.

"Who?"

"Don't play coy with me. You have Josh here somewhere."

"Cole?" Annie asked, frightened not by Mitch's belligerent attitude but by his words and the extreme worry etched in Cole's eyes.

"Josh's jacket, gloves and boots are gone."

15

"WHERE IS HE? DID HE HELP YOU WITH YOUR FAVOR-garnering cider gig after all?" Mitch said.

Annie took a step back from his accusation.

"Mitch, that's enough," Cole said, moving between them.

"Stand up for your son, Cole, and stop protecting this little slut. It's her fault."

Annie saw Cole's fists clench and Mitch's eyes narrow. Putting her fingers to her mouth, she whistled. That stopped both men's bickering. "Josh is missing?"

At Cole's miserable nod, Annie's stomach dropped. It was snowing, nearly zero degrees and the streets would be deserted soon, leaving very few people who might have spotted him to ask. "Have you called the police?"

"No, he hasn't, because I know he's here."

The snarl Mitch directed her way was painful. He was out of control, and Annie felt empathy for him, even as he was venting all his anger and grief in the wrong direction. "Feel free to look, but I'm sure he left with you."

"Wait," Cole held up his hand. "I remember I heard something, like a sob. I turned around and your front door was still ajar."

"When?"

"While we were having our discussion."

"You don't think he heard us, do you?"

"It's possible."

Annie groaned. If Josh had heard her say she couldn't be their mother, it could have sounded to young ears as if she were rejecting him. It sounded that way to her ears.

And she had no idea if Josh would have understood when she'd told Cole it had nothing to do with him or the boys, that it was her issue.

Nausea flooded into her stomach and burned her throat. What a stupid, selfish thing to say. Why couldn't she have stopped to think and not blurt out the first thing that fear popped into her head?

"He's not here. Look if you want; meanwhile call the police. Where's Peter?"

"At home," Cole said.

"He's got to be scared. Mitch, why don't you go back and sit with him," Annie suggested.

"I'm going to look for Josh. Cole can sit with him. Anyway, as Josh's father, the police will want to question him."

Mitch made it sound like Cole was at fault.

"Stop being a jerk, Mitch. This is a time for family to pull together, not tear each other apart," she said.

Annie paid no more attention to Mitch's posturing. He wasn't helping anything. "Cole, do you think once the police have all the information, that Peter will let me stay with him while you and Mitch start searching."

"I told you, I'm leaving now—"

"Then go already," Annie interrupted Mitch.

"To answer your question," Cole said. "I think Peter will be happy to have you there."

Annie ran to the kitchen, and grabbed the plate of cookies, then snagged her jacket and cell phone and locked the door behind her.

"Where's Uncle Mitch?" Peter asked, his voice small and scared, after Cole and Annie entered the living room sans Mitch.

Cole hugged his son and kissed his hair. "He's gone to start looking for Josh."

"Josh is too small to be out there," Peter said, his voice tight.

Peter moved out of his arms and stared at the cold, empty fireplace. It needed a fire, Cole thought. Something homey and warm for when Josh came home. "Listen, while we're waiting for the police, how about if we build a fire for Josh?"

Peter set the kindling as Cole stacked the wood. Annie handed Peter a long match. It flamed on the second strike, and Cole watched as his eldest son carefully held the wavering flame to one spot of kindling until it took and then moved to the next.

When had he learned to light a fire?

Annie sat heavily on the couch and patted the cushion next to her. After only a moment of hesitation, Peter sat where she'd indicated, his eyes wide with fear.

Cole realized Annie hadn't said a word since coming into his house, yet words weren't necessary as Peter inched closer to her. She radiated confidence, just what Peter needed.

Yet when their glances met, he saw the same anxiety mirrored in her eyes. She was holding herself together for Peter's sake.

Damn if his sons didn't need a mother in their lives. And Annie had rejected them all.

No, that's not true, at least be honest. Annie has lived under a misconception for too long.

Cole wondered if he'd have the chance to show her she was wrong about herself. Then the doorbell rang.

Moments later, Cole was ushering two of Boulder's finest into the living room.

He answered their questions and handed them a school photo of his little boy. They left after calling in a BOLO for Josh.

Cole sagged against the living room doors. This was out of his control. Just like Lauren's illness.

But at least this time he could do something: get in the car and start canvassing the streets.

Mitch had said he was going south of Baseline, Columbine, Mariposa, Bluebell and King from

Chautauqua to Broadway. Cole would start on 20th Street from Baseline to Broadway all way up to 6th Street, then the hilly Willowbrook and Circle Drive. His little boy couldn't have gone farther than that.

Pulling on gloves and a hat, he was ready to head out.

"I've got the cell phone, so I'll call yours, leaving the land line open for the police."

Peter jumped up and ran into the kitchen, coming back with a baggie into which he stuffed Annie's cookies.

"Dad, Josh'll be hungry."

Cole hugged Peter tight against him and felt Peter's good arm hug him back.

Turning to leave, Cole whirled around and glanced at Annie.

Tears glistened in her eyes, and she moved to stand next to Peter.

Cole touched her lips with his finger. "We'll find him."

"Okay, I'll tell Peter." Annie pushed the button to disconnect Cole's call on her cell phone.

"That was your dad. He's on 9th Street now. So far no sign of Josh, and Uncle Mitch hasn't seen any sign of him yet."

Peter glanced toward her as she spoke, then turned back to stare out the large living room window.

Annie ached that she couldn't fix this for him, that she couldn't go and hug him as he stood alone, so scared.

Unable to watch Peter suffer, she left the couch and

moved the short distance to stand beside him. Not touching him, but there if he needed her.

"He said he was beginning to forget her and as much as he loved you and hoped you'd be our new mom, he didn't want to forget Mom."

Peter's words were rough with tears.

"Peter, can you tell me a bit more about what Josh meant?"

"Josh has been saying he wanted to find a star that would always remind him of Mom. He hadn't mentioned it in a few days because I kinda got the feeling he thought you might be our new mom."

Annie's throat thickened with tears she wouldn't let fall in front of Peter.

Then he nearly broke her as he leaned against her. She pulled him close as they both stared into the night, the falling snow highlighted by the lights in her back yard.

Annie blinked as a huge star came into focus.

The enormous star on Flagstaff Mountain, lit for all of Boulder to see. Was it possible that Josh had gone there? It was a hike, but he could have gone up Flagstaff Road, then trekked up the meadow to reach it.

She'd done the hike many times, and it was a good quick workout in the summer; but it was winter and Josh was only seven years old.

"Peter grab your outdoor stuff, including a hat."

He didn't say a word as he scattered to do Annie's bidding.

She punched in Cole's number and waited what seemed like minutes before he picked up.

"I think I know where Josh could be. Meet me at the first turnout on Flagstaff."

She punched off the phone. "Peter, grab some blankets, get them off the bed if you need to," she said. "Let's roll."

16

COLE'S HONDA WAS ALREADY AT THE FIRST OVERLOOK ON Flagstaff, and Mitch pulled in right after Annie.

"The parking area is past the Flagstaff House on the left. Then we'll hike to the star. It's steep and slippery."

She'd really hoped they'd find Josh before this point.

Annie led the caravan of SUVs to the next turnout. It was easy to see the star from here once the lights were on, but that was the only easy part.

They crossed the road and started hiking in. Annie swept her flashlight back and forth, illuminating the surrounding trees and boulders. Mitch and Cole were doing the same.

"Josh? Call out so we can find you," Cole yelled repeatedly.

Annie thought she saw footprints, now nearly buried in the fresh snow, and followed them. Her light caught a small figure in a bright blue parka huddled against a pine tree, the lit star still a distance away up the hill.

"Josh?" Annie slogged as fast as she could through the calf-high snow, its bulk slowing each step. "Josh, we're here."

Annie fell to her knees and gathered Josh tight against her. Seconds later Cole was next to her, and she handed his son over to him.

"Son, why did you do this? You scared us all so badly." Cole wrapped Josh in a bear hug.

"I heard you and Annie fighting and her tell you that she didn't want to be our mommy. If Annie couldn't be our mom, then I needed a star to look at so I'd have Mommy close by. I thought this big star would help me find the right one."

Annie brushed the snow from his woolen hat, caressed his frozen cheek and looked into his cold-pinched face. God, what if they hadn't gotten here in time? "Oh, sweetie, I'm so sorry you heard that, and I'm sorry I said it."

Cole glanced up at her, his expression neutral.

Pain ballooned in her heart. Josh left the warmth and security of his home and family because of something she said, and Cole's love for her had been extinguished by her hastily uttered words.

"I wanted you to be our new mommy, but you don't love us, Annie." Tears ran down his reddened and chapped cheeks.

Mitch shoved in closer, nearly pushing her over. "Josh, you have us to love you right here, right now. You don't need anyone else," he said.

"Hey, Josh, don't forget it was Annie who found you. She was really worried about you, so maybe someday she'll love us," Peter said, patting his brother on the back while sending Mitch a glare.

There wasn't enough room under the tree for all of them, so Annie clambered to her feet and backed away.

Standing outside the circle of family huddled together, Peter's words wouldn't leave her mind. *Maybe someday she'll love us.*

She already did. Josh and Peter and Cole had captured her heart, which is exactly why she couldn't chance the pain that would follow if—

Wait a minute, Annie girl. Aren't you already hurting? Too late.

You're rejecting them so they won't reject you first.

She stood glued to the spot as the truth of her words poured through her. She'd blown this chance and was pretty sure she'd not get another one.

Her attention returned to the group as Cole hefted Josh. "Let's get you home. Annie has blankets in the car to warm you up."

They trekked back through the deepening snow to the shelter of their cars. Cole carrying Josh, Peter beside him, carefully lighting the way with the flashlight his father had handed him, and touching Josh as if to make sure he was okay.

Mitch followed them and Annie brought up the rear.

Cole put Josh in the front seat of his car and started it, blasting the heat. Luckily it was still warm from the driving done while searching for Josh in the neighborhood, but he still shivered as Cole tucked the blanket around him.

Annie again brought up the rear as the three SUVs snaked down the steep icy road.

Two vehicles pulled into Cole's driveway and Annie pulled into hers.

She watched as the man she loved carried Josh inside, followed closely by Mitch. Peter paused at the doorway and waved to her, then ducked inside.

Cole's family was all together, safe under one roof. This was family time and she wasn't part of it.

COLE CALLED THE POLICE TO INFORM THEM THEY'D FOUND Josh and that he was cold but fine, and the police removed the BOLO. He and Mitch took turns sitting with Josh in case he woke with a nightmare, but his son slept soundly. Glancing at the clock by Josh's bed, Cole realized it was nearly midnight.

Treading softly, Cole left the room, went into his bedroom and looked out the window. Annie's light was still on.

Heading down the creaky stairs, vowing to fix them next week, Cole stepped into the living room where Mitch was catnapping on the couch.

A couple of things had to be solved before midnight, and Mitch was either going to agree or be severely restricted in his access to the boys. Cole wouldn't forbid him to see them, that would hurt the boys, but there would be family outings that would, with luck and his power of persuasion, include Annie.

He touched Mitch gently on the shoulder, and the man was instantly awake. "Would you mind sitting with Josh for a while? I need to go over and thank Annie for finding Josh."

"You love her, don't you?"

"Yes, I do, but, and this should make you happy, there's only a slim chance that it will go anywhere. Nevertheless, I'm going to try."

Mitch stared at the Christmas tree for a long moment as Cole braced himself for another nasty exchange.

"It's going to be hard you know, watching you and Annie, watching the boys love her, knowing it should be Lauren here instead."

"Mitch, if it hadn't been for the boys and you, I'd have crawled into my science and become a bitter, lonely man.

"Loving Annie doesn't mean my memories of Lauren vanish. Nor do I want the boys to forget their mother. I want them to remember her in a healthy way, not with the angry grief you still harbor. It isn't healthy for them or, frankly, for you."

"Are you giving me an ultimatum?"

"Not really. I'm trying to make you see that what you're doing is hurting everyone. And I think Lauren would be the first to say so.

"If you don't want to stay with Josh, I won't thank Annie until tomorrow, but I will thank her, and if I can find a way to bring her into this family, I will."

"It's going to be hard."

Cole closed his eyes in relief. "I know, but you'll have us every step of the way."

I'M STANDING OUTSIDE YOUR DOOR. WILL YOU LET ME IN, please?

Annie read Cole's text twice.

Then flew down the stairs and opened the door.

Cole stood there, one hand behind his back.

"Merry Christmas."

Then he handed her what he'd been hiding, a beautifully wrapped box.

She pulled him inside. "Are you crazy? It's nearly midnight—you could have waited until morning to come over."

"I think I am crazy, and I didn't want to wait until morning to find out for sure. We need to talk. And just so you know, I asked Mitch to sit with Josh while I was over here. Mitch agreed and Josh is sleeping soundly. None the worse for his ordeal."

"I'm so terribly sorry about Josh. It scares me to think what could have happened—"

"But didn't, thanks to you."

"If he hadn't overheard—"

"I know and that's an interesting problem, but before we go into it, do you have any wine? And it's a bit dark in here. How about a fire and turning on the Christmas tree?" Cole asked.

"I wasn't much in the mood for Christmas—"

"But now you have to unwrap that," he said, pointing to the gift she held. "And you can't do that in front of a dark Christmas tree."

A bubble of laughter escaped her lips and darn if it didn't feel good after the drama going on since early evening. "Okay, after the wine. Pinot grigio or pinot noir?"

"Grigio."

She poured two glasses, led the way into the living room, and motioned for Cole to sit on the couch.

"It's still dark in here."

"Just wait." Picking up a remote, she pressed a button and the tree lit up, pushed another button and the fire flamed to life.

"Nifty tricks. I'm going to have to do that with my house."

Those two words, *my house,* brought back the real meaning of his visit. She took a large gulp of wine and nearly choked as her throat tightened up.

"What did you want to talk about?" She was quite sure she didn't really want to know, but he was here and she'd pretend for a moment all was good between them.

"First, unwrap the present."

"Cole—"

"Please."

Annie carefully slid off the gold ribbon, then peeled back the red paper from each end and finally the middle. Opening the box, she unfolded the tissue paper to find the cashmere shawl she'd so admired at the Italian clothing store where they'd stopped to pick up Jen's earrings.

She buried her face in it, then held it out to Cole.

"You don't like it?" he asked, obviously taken aback.

"No, no, I love it. I just want you to put it on me."

Annie sat still as Cole leaned forward and draped the

ultra soft cashmere around her, looping the ends into a gentle knot over her chest.

"How's that?"

"Perfect. Thank you. It's an elegant gift, but really you—"

"Yes, I should have. And you're welcome."

Annie looked at him, wishing she could capture this moment and hold it forever. But he'd mentioned a problem, so she had to the face the music. She figured Cole realized she was right and they weren't meant to have a life together, and the shawl was now a goodbye present.

She sucked in a deep breath. "What was the problem you mentioned?"

"I wanted to talk about Josh—"

She couldn't help it, the breath she'd taken exhaled in a rush of pure relief. "You know, you said nearly that same thing the first time we sat in this room."

Annie recalled the memory as they drank peppermint lattes in her living room, the first meeting that began the thaw between them.

"I remember it quite clearly."

The desire in Cole's eyes filled her with a heat neither the fire nor the wine could match.

Maybe he wasn't saying goodbye, maybe he was going for the friends-with-benefits idea. *But now I don't want to.*

"Josh did overhear our conversation, but that wasn't your fault, so don't take on any guilt over it. He shouldn't have been listening, but he's seven and I understand his being upset. I was upset. I didn't like what I was hearing.

"So, I want you to please explain why you don't want to

be a mother to Josh and Peter and a wife and lover to me? I want the real answer this time."

He set down his glass and lifted the glass from her suddenly nerveless hands, then intertwined their fingers.

"If it's because you don't love me, I guess I can accept that, but since we live next door to each other, you're easy to reach. I warn you, I'll keep trying to change your mind."

She looked at their fingers, joined with little space between them. It was symbolic of what she thought love should be between two people. Lives intertwined, yet the fingers were attached to two individual people who would grow together. She let loose a sigh.

"Rejection. My mother rejected my father and me. So did some of my married friends who were having children and were uncomfortable around me now that I was sterile. I was depressed and felt as if I had the plague all of a sudden. I had no control over any of it."

"Annie, you said you were deeply depressed about your hysterectomy. Do you think that's the reason people shied away from you? I honestly don't think it was because you were sterile. Most people don't know how to react around people who are ill or depressed."

She looked at him uncertainly. "But then there was Ralph Holt—I told you about him."

"Yes, and thankfully he was an idiot."

Cole's meaning dawned on Annie and she grinned, hope beginning to light a tiny flame in her heart. But first she had to know the answer to the question that had nagged her most.

"How many kids do you want, Cole?"

"The two I have, unless you want to adopt."

"Really?"

"Yeah, really. I've always believed in the concept of zero population growth, replacing ourselves with the same number of kids, but there are a lot of kids out there who need loving homes. So, if you want to grow the family and the boys are okay with it, we'll grow the family."

Tears began to trickle down her cheek, but she wouldn't break the bond of their fingers just yet to wipe them away. "I don't want to hurt the boys the way I was hurt when my mother left us, and if you change your mind later about wanting biological kids—"

"Why would I change my mind?"

"Because you wanted a houseful of kids."

"Lauren wanted a houseful of her own kids. It was one of the few differences we argued over." He kissed their entwined fingers. "Annie, I want to finish my life with you by my side. Josh adores you and Peter is close to being there also."

"And I love the boys."

"But?"

"What about Mitch?"

Cole groaned. "I hope, after the discussion he and I had tonight, that he will be coming to terms with the fact that you're in our lives for keeps and that you're not an ogre or the evil queen, you're sweet Annie who has put us three Evans men under your spell."

"And now who's the storyteller?"

"It's only the truth."

"I guess it's okay then to tell you I love you with all my heart."

His sigh of relief said it all.

Annie pulled him closer and touched her lips gently to his. There would be time for fast and hard later. This was the moment to seal their lives, soft and slow.

"I agree."

"Mind reading again?"

"Hopefully always. So I take it, you'll be mine this Christmas night?" Cole asked against her lips.

"Always." And she sealed her promise with another soft kiss.

~ The End ~

LETTER TO MY READERS

Dear Reader,

The lit star on Boulder's Flagstaff Mountain is real. It's been lit at Christmas since I was a young child.

This story came about one snowy night as I was sitting in my office watching the snow fall and talking to my mother on the phone, telling her how much I still looked forward to seeing the star every season.

She told me a story about an incident at a neighborhood party where a man was grousing about the star and how it was too Christian to be used. Mom looked at him and said that she never thought about it being particularly religious in tone, but more a symbol of hope and light.

Thus my story was born. Annie lives in approximately the same distance from the star that I do, and the same proximity to Chautauqua Park. Guess what, I have the tall Linden tree in my front yard!

The series happened when I had quite a few readers

contact me and tell me they wanted more from the characters.

Incredibly exciting stuff for an author to hear.

If you enjoyed this story, please leave a review on the store's review site where you purchased it. And if you can at BookBub and Goodreads as well. We writers live or die by reviews. I know it sounds dramatic but it is so true. This is the way readers find us and buy the book.

Also, on my website www.lesliesartor.com, you can find entire *Star Light ~ Star Bright* series on the "Book Shelf" page.

And I have a newsletter that enjoy writing and sending monthly. Keeping you up to date on my writing, my crazy busy life and often my photography. And don't forget, I love hearing from you via email!

ACKNOWLEDGMENTS

No writer works completely alone. While we do spend hours in our own head, creating characters, conflict, romance and suspense, there are real people we turn to and depend on.

My Beta Readers, Audra Harders, Christine Dunning, Jessie Peiker and Nina Victor.
Thank you for your patience and your insight—you made my book that much better.

My editor, Ellis Vidler, who has great story sense and a mastery of the English language. Thank you for continually making me better at my craft.

My Cover Guru, Neringa, who worked to make me proficient at Photoshop.

ALSO BY L.A. SARTOR

STAR LIGHT ~ STAR BRIGHT

A Romantic Christmas Series Set In Snowy Boulder, Colorado

Be Mine This Christmas Night

Forever Yours This New Year's Night

Believe In Me This Christmas Morn

Dream Of Me This Christmas Eve

THE CARSWELL ADVENTURE SERIES

Heart Pounding Adventure & Romance Set In Exotic Locales

Stone Of Heaven

Viking Gold

THE KAHUNA GROUP

Romantic Suspense With Powerful, Professional Investigators-
Offices in Hawaii ~ Denver ~ Los Angeles

Dare To Believe

Brushed By Betrayal

THE PLANTATION SERIES

Pure Romance Set in Costa Rica On A Rare Cacao Plantation

Prince Of Granola

THE JENNA HART MYSTERIES

A Cozy Mystery Series Set in the Colorado Ski Town Of
Angelcroft

Tick Tock Dead (coming soon)

*Capture the code with a mobile device's QR reader to see all
of L.A. Sartor's Books*

ABOUT THE AUTHOR

I started writing as a child, really. A few things happened on the way to becoming a published author ... specifically, a junior high school teacher who told me I couldn't write because I didn't want to study grammar.

That English teacher stopped my writing for years. But the muse couldn't be denied, and eventually I wrote, a lot, some of it award winning.

My husband told me repeatedly that independent publishing was becoming a valid way to publish a novel. I didn't believe him. I thought indie meant vanity press.

I couldn't have been more wrong.

I started pursuing this direction seriously, hit the keyboard, learned a litany of new things and published my first novel. My second book became a bestseller, and I'm absolutely on the right course in my life.

I live in Colorado with my husband Gary whom I met on a blind date—I can't imagine life without my best friend. We play in the mountains and travel as much as possible.

Find me at www.lesliesartor.com

FOREVER YOURS THIS NEW YEAR'S NIGHT

STAR LIGHT ~ STAR BRIGHT SERIES
BOOK TWO

CHAPTER 1

"WE HAVE MET, I'M WOUNDED YOU DON'T REMEMBER."

Jennifer Malone looked up from her bowl of fettuccine Alfredo. The same man who'd fed her that lame "haven't we met" pickup line while she was waiting in the bar for her table, had returned. "I thought I made it fairly clear I wasn't interested."

He stood way too close to her chair for comfort. She dropped her gaze, not wanting to lead him on. Damn, dining alone shouldn't make her a target for his advances. Especially not in this elegant restaurant high above Washington, DC.

"Are you still a sore loser, or is it that you really don't remember me?"

Pulling her thoughts together, Jen looked put down her fork and looked closely at the man in front of her. Tall, dark and way too handsome, this guy was someone she wouldn't have easily forgotten. His gray eyes held the hint of a private joke, his lips curving up on one side as if amused by their encounter.

A shadow of a name passed her mind, but no way could he be the same person.

She squinted and realized with a sick jolt that, although he wore his hair longer and had a five o'clock shadow most movie stars would envy, he was the same man.

Major Brice Young, who was a major jerk. She smiled at her own pun, then quickly put on her serious game face.

"Regrettably, I recall our last meeting all too clearly." She put as much displeasure as she could into those three words. *That should do it.*

Instead, he laughed, taking her off guard. Most men would have taken the hint and left her alone the first time she'd brushed them off and not come back for more. But he had the guts to laugh at her.

"Hey, it wasn't my fault your side lost the case. Your guy had money to hire the best expert witness, and that was you. But he shouldn't have tried to hack the Air Force and then find a bad hacker to cover his tracks. You didn't have a chance."

Then Major Young pulled out the other chair at her table, moved it closer to her and sat.

"Don't hate me. I was just doing my job," he said.

Jen didn't notice any hint of contrition in his voice. Arrogant dude. But then, she'd thought the same thing at the trial.

She refused to be intimidated by him and have her dinner ruined She sipped from her wine glass, twirled more fettuccine on her fork and chewed slowly as he watched silently. She took another small bite and still he watched without a word.

Jen put her fork down and glared at him, hoping her tactic worked and she didn't have to resort to calling over the maître d'.

Instead of removing himself or quailing under her glare, he laughed again. A deep, rich, way-too-enticing laugh, which would work on 99.9 percent of the female population. She, however, was the other 0.1 percent.

"Jennifer Malone, perhaps you do deserve your nickname, Madame Ice Queen." He shivered dramatically. "But frankly, that frozen attitude isn't working here, not for me anyway."

He grabbed the bottle of Merlot on the table, looked at the label, picked up her glass, gave it a sniff, and took a sip.

Jen couldn't help it—her eyes widened and a gasp escaped.

"Good choice. Nice whisper of black cherry."

Handing her back the glass, she automatically took a sip to see if he was right.

He was. And before she could wipe her mouth of the droplet she felt clinging to her lips, he wiped it away with his finger.

Then licked the droplet off said finger. "Was I right?"

"Yes."

His grin grew wider with a hint of wickedness that sent a quiver of erotic arrows deep into her body. Pushing back his chair, Major Brice Young winked at her, then walked out of the restaurant with an easy gait.

Damn him. On so many levels.

She wasn't on the losing end of many cases, her expert witness testimony was just that, expert. But somehow the evidence had been tampered with and the Major had found the exchange of data. Her client got slammed with an enormous fine and a PR nightmare. Government one, Jen zero, and she was a bad loser.

And how she hated that moniker, Madame Ice Queen. She wasn't. She had feelings, hot, cold, anger, love, and lust, like any other person. She just kept them tucked away. It was a defensive strategy for her business, and usually it worked quite well.

Jen picked up the wine glass and drank deeply, realizing as she did that her lips touched the same spot as his, and another arrow found its mark deep inside her.

Really? On Christmas Eve she was having a stab of lust for a man she despised? *You know, you really are a bad loser. Despise? That's a bit strong.*

Dislike?

Better.

Pushing away her plate of cooling pasta, Jen stared out of the enormous windows of the restaurant spanning the upper two floors of the hotel. Atop the distant Washington Monument, red beacons flashed in the freshly falling snow. She looked down to see that the Washington Mall was all but deserted and Jen realized she was homesick.

The frequent traveling was beginning to drag on her. With the anonymous hotels, meetings in concrete office buildings and countless courtrooms she visited all over the country, everything blurred together into a dreary shade of beige.

Refusing dessert, Jen signed her room number to the bill and headed down two floors to her suite.

After kicking off her black stilettos and yanking off her blouse and black pencil skirt, she pulled back the covers and lay on the soft white sheets, still wearing the scraps of lace that passed for her undies. Glancing at the time on her cell phone, she saw with a pang that it was past midnight on the east coast. Christmas Day at this end of the country.

Instead of being 1400 miles away, Jen should be back in Boulder, Colorado, celebrating Christmas Eve as usual with her best buddy, Annie Hamilton.

They'd be sitting in front of Annie's Christmas tree decorated with a gazillion lights, with her eclectic, treasured ornaments bending every bough.

Annie would have lit the fire, its flames creating tranquility as they reflected off the crushed glass beneath them.

And instead of hotel fare, they'd be noshing on Annie's famous homemade fettuccine Alfredo, wine glasses close at hand, and the bottle within easy reach.

What was her best bud doing right now? Was she with Cole, her new next-door neighbor, and his boys? Jen had met Cole, and Annie couldn't have fallen for a better guy. Now if she'd just realize he was the *right* guy.

"Merry Christmas, Annie. I hope it's perfect for you. Sweet dreams," she whispered into the ether.

Jen knew she should get some sleep before this

mysterious meeting tomorrow, but whether she closed or eyes or stared at the ceiling, the image of Major Brice Young's face played in front of her.

Dark gray eyes with flecks of gold, almost eerie in their color. Lips that sucked that droplet of wine. A chin that said Brice brooked no resistance. And what was with the long hair that curled at the nape of his neck, in stark contrast with his crisp white shirt? Not military hair for sure.

Madame Ice Queen.

Jen closed her eyes against the burn of tears, refusing to let a single one fall as she replayed the sting in Brice's voice. She was strong, independent, and she wasn't an Ice Queen. She wasn't.

Once again, she wished she were home.

Damn, but Jennifer Malone was a frozen woman, albeit a stunning "Madame Ice Queen."

Brice had approached her with the intent of giving her a head's up about tomorrow's meeting and how important it was for him to have her there. Knowing she wouldn't be keen about being around him at all, he planned all his arguments to win her over.

Then, after her first rebuff in the bar, his contrary streak challenged him to find out if she had a heart that pumped blood and not ice water under that white blouse.

And now, freezing in the parking lot of the hotel, scraping the ice off his car, he smiled grimly. Glacial water ran through her veins, and she was just going to have to find out the punch line of tomorrow's meeting, at the meeting.

Wounded ego, eh, man?

Perhaps, but there was no denying the flood of plain old desire that had surged through him as he'd followed his knee-jerk impulse to wipe that droplet off her lip.

He shouldn't have done it. Plain and simple.

Yet, for a brief second, he thought he saw fire in her gaze. And that enticed him. If he could only figure out how to make it happen again.

Man, you've got enough on your plate without adding skirt chasing. Besides, you're still singed from Bethany.

All true, he acknowledged to his inner voice. One he should listen to more often. It had warned him about his ex-wife, but he'd been too deafened by the attention she lavished on him and, heck, the hot sex, to hear a word of it.

Anyway, this project was too important and time too short to do anything other than work.

Too bad for Miss Jennifer Malone, who could use the thawing.

Brice entered his small, and supposedly temporary apartment, though he'd been living here a year. Not bothering to flip on the lights, he dodged his cheap futon couch and laminated coffee table. With a few strides he crossed to the sliding glass door fronting his pitifully small balcony.

He watched the white crystals drift down, piling on the deck's railing, and hoped the flimsy thing would hold up under the snow's weight.

And damn, in his haste to get to the hotel's restaurant, he'd forgotten to turn up the heat. Drafts of cold air puffed through the ancient window's seals. Brice pulled his wool scarf tight and kept on his overcoat while he stared at the bleakness and beauty of the scene in front of him.

Had he made the right choice retiring from the military? The money from this new venture could be astronomical, and he'd get his retirement pay on top of that. He could work his own hours. Especially now that Bethany was out of the picture, always demanding that her social and shopping needs be met during his off-duty time.

One separation painful, the other not.

His marriage had been short-lived, and all he felt now was relief.

But his time in the Air Force was more than his job—it had been his life, and that seemed played out as well.

All in all, both splits seemed right, or in the case of Bethany, more than right. Resuming bachelorhood hadn't been all that hard if you didn't count the accommodations.

Being a civvie? Well, that was going to be damn hard.

Finally, he turned from the window and headed into his bedroom. A sleeper compartment on a train had more space. It didn't take him long to pack his bag, he wasn't going to be gone more than a week. Then stripping quickly, he pulled on clean but well-worn sweats. He set the alarm, knowing he'd get the evil eye from the General if he was late to the meeting tomorrow. And finally slipped into his cold bed.

Then he couldn't get that one fiery flash from Jennifer

Malone out of his brain. Beautiful and smart. *Don't forget tough as nails.*

Well, he was used to tough. Just wait, there were going to be some sparks that had nothing to do with physical attraction. This project was too important to blow and he would brook no interference.

Brice smiled as sleep began to claim him.

JEN FOLLOWED HER ESCORT THROUGH THE UTILITARIAN corridors of the Pentagon, swearing she'd never again work on Christmas Day.

She paused outside the meeting room door to straighten her black sweater and smooth her black slim skirt. Wrapping the red scarf around her neck a bit tighter, she glanced down her black tight-clad legs and smiled at her other spot of bright holiday color, her red shorty boots. It was Christmas, and if she wanted to wear red, then fine.

The officer who'd escorted her flashed her a smile. "Love the boots," she said. "Ready?"

"Ready. And thanks, they were a whim, but I love 'em too."

The officer opened the door.

Her overcoat folded over one arm and laptop case in her other hand, Jen entered the room, confidence beaming from every pore. As usual for the Pentagon, she found a room full of men in uniform.

And thankfully, there wasn't a single Major Brice Young in the group.

When the Pentagon asked her to be *the* beta tester of a new system their brightest cyber geek had just finished, she was intrigued.

And when the general named a figure and, in the same breath, asked if she could be here in a day, she was hooked. You just didn't turn down a job like this, and anyway, she liked working in tandem with the brains in the military. They didn't often come onto her, and stars on any shoulders didn't faze her.

Nor did being the only woman in the room. Well, it honestly bothered her that there weren't other women included in the ranks of the men before her, but not being the only female in the room.

"Gentlemen," she said as they moved forward almost as a unit. *Ah, military precision.*

After shaking hands, she took her seat, opened her laptop. Then waited.

The men were still standing. She counted, added herself and realized there was one extra chair.

"Sorry, sir. Snarl on the 110."

Jen closed her eyes. No bloody way could this happen. *Damn and double damn.*

"And Ms. Malone, glad to see you made it here safely."

Jen nodded, settling her face into a serene expression. 'I had a driver, courtesy of General Cartwright."

Everyone sat. The general cleared his throat and drew all eyes, except hers.

She snuck a peek at Brice, only to see his grin while his eyes remained front and center.

And he didn't have on a uniform. What was going on?

"We want Vader to be on line in the next ten days," the General said.

Vader? She'd heard of this Vader. The name was the scuttlebutt in the industry, but no one knew anything about it.

"And the testing is to be done by you, Ms. Malone. Mr. Young is going to throw everything he can at the system. We want to know if Vader can block cyber attacks and track who is responsible for said attacks."

She was going to get to test Vader?

Jen would have done it for free just to see how it worked. *Merry Christmas to me.*

Now she looked directly at Brice only to see that his grin, while still there, had a weary look to it. Nor was she wrong last night. He did have dark smudges under his eyes. "Mr. Young? What happened to Major Young?" she blurted out.

"Retired after my twenty."

"Yes, damn him," General Cartwright added. "Dangling the rank of Lieutenant Colonel wasn't enough to keep him in longer."

She'd thought Brice would have been a general some day. He had the attitude when he presented his evidence at the trial. Tearing apart the one bit of cyber evidence that she and her employee, Todd Sargent, had been leery about.

Todd hated the major with a passion and despised losing as much as she did. "I'm guessing you and I are going to be working together testing Vader?" she asked Brice.

He nodded, and his grin grew wider.

"Why you?" Vader or not, why did this particular man have to be the one she was to be partnered with?

"Vader is my baby, and I need to watch it grow up."

He designed Vader? Holy moly. This guy must be brilliant.

Suddenly, she felt as if she were back in the "slow group" during elementary school. She wasn't stupid, hadn't been then, but she had been bored. To tears. She'd hated school until Doc Hamilton suggested the principal move her into his daughter, Annie's, class, a grade ahead. Then she began to excel, proving her surrogate father was dead right.

She shook off the memory. It needed to be erased, but somehow it always cropped up when she was being tested. She reminded herself that she was as smart as Brice Young, and she'd prove it to him.

"I test in *my* lab," she said, making the snap decision while keeping her voice flat to cover her excitement over this new challenge. She needed to be on her turf to make sure she had all *her* tools right at her fingertips.

"That's fine. I like Colorado."

"Are you bringing along a ton of equipment?"

"Nope. Laptop, tablet, Vader, some clothes and me. Vader isn't small, but it's portable."

"Good. I assume we'll connect it to the public Internet?"

"Yup, I've got some very interesting attack scenarios, and you're going to tell me what gets through and how."

"Maybe even why."

"You're that good?"

"Isn't that why you wanted me?" Jen asked with a sudden spurt of confidence.

"So, I gather we're set, Ms. Malone?" the general asked.

"Yes, sir."

"Good, then let's get started. Clock's ticking. I'll call Andrews and tell them that you're on your way, while you pick up your gear at the hotel. You'll head home courtesy of the Air Force."

Brice started to salute, then stuck out his hand to General Cartwright, who clasped it warmly. It was obvious to Jen the two were close and, she'd guess, could now afford to show it. They stood by the door, waiting for her.

Jen shook the general's hand. "It'll be a pleasure to test Vader, General. Thank you for allowing me this fun."

"Not my idea, though I liked it. It was his." The general nodded to Major Brice Young, retired.

www.ingramcontent.com/pod-product-compliance
Lightning Source LLC
Chambersburg PA
CBHW020244150626
46552CB00020B/159